DANTE'S TRIUMPH

COLLEEN LEBERE

Dante's Triumph

Copyright © 2017 by Colleen LeBere

No part of this publication may be reproduced, distributed, or transmitted in any form or by any means, including photocopying, recording, or other electronic or mechanical methods, without the prior written permission of the author, except in the case of brief quotations embodied in critical reviews and certain other non-commercial uses permitted by copyright law.

Tellwell Talent
www.tellwell.ca

ISBN
978-1-77370-483-8 (Paperback)
978-1-77370-484-5 (eBook)

TABLE OF CONTENTS

Prologue.. vii

CHAPTER ONE..1
    GETTING STARTED

CHAPTER TWO..5
    SURPRISE ARRIVAL

CHAPTER THREE.....................................13
    MERRIN GOES TO ITALY

CHAPTER FOUR......................................21
    MERRIN'S VISIT TO SASKATCHEWAN

CHAPTER FIVE......................................31
    TRAGIC ACCIDENT

CHAPTER SIX.......................................47
    THE AKIRA FAMILY

CHAPTER SEVEN.....................................53
    IN REGARDS TO THE CHILDREN

CHAPTER EIGHT.....................................61
    BACK TO PROVIDENCE!

CHAPTER NINE......................................65
    BASEBALL AND ELVIS

CHAPTER TEN.......................................69
    GRADUATION AND GOODBYE

CHAPTER ELEVEN....................................75
    THE ITALIANS VISIT

CHAPTER TWELVE....................................83
    THE BANK BOOKS!

CHAPTER THIRTEEN..................................89
    TROUBLE IN MISSOULA

CHAPTER FOURTEEN................................97
    GRADUATION AND CONCERNS

CHAPTER FIFTEEN 105
    SECRET PLANS

CHAPTER SIXTEEN 115
    CERTAIN ADJUSTMENTS

CHAPTER SEVENTEEN.............................. 121
    HOME FROM THE DODGERS

CHAPTER EIGHTEEN 129
    ITALY AND THE VILLA

CHAPTER NINETEEN 135
    MEETING THE FAMILY

CHAPTER TWENTY.................................143
    RESTORING THE VILLA

CHAPTER TWENTY-ONE...........................149
    DANTE TRAVELS

CHAPTER TWENTY-TWO 157
    HOME FOR A FUNERAL

CHAPTER TWENTY-THREE 161
    CONFRONTING OLIVIA

CHAPTER TWENTY-FOUR 169
    CAPPI GEONNA

CHAPTER TWENTY-FIVE 175
    ALL ABOUT LUCA!

CHAPTER TWENTY-SIX............................. 181
    A SCOUT FROM THE YANKEES

CHAPTER TWENTY-SEVEN 185
    A TRIP TO NEW YORK

CHAPTER TWENTY-EIGHT.......................... 191
    ANOTHER LOVE STORY

DEDICATION

Dedicated to my husband Wayne,
and your love of baseball!
Your story was such a major part of this book.
Thanks Wayne!

To my family!

Mark and Lorene, Megan

Leo and Ashlee, Eden, Maddox and Viola

Paul and Donna, Kate and Reed

Alex and Erin, Alexa, Payton and Ava

Special thanks to you Mark, for inspiring
me to finish the book and your input
in regards to the game!

PROLOGUE

DANTE CASTRINNI SAT ASTRIDE HIS HORSE, FOUR WINDS, AND viewed the Villa Val di Pesa and the surrounding countryside. A soft wind blew through his curly black hair, as he looked over his workmanship. He admired how the faded yellow walls of the Villa contrasted with the bright burgundy shutters. Past the tall Cypress trees bordering the driveway, he could see the sparkling water in the swimming pool, the stables, the pasture for the horses, and the baseball field which he and his friend Rom had recently constructed.

It was a panoramic view of his heart's desires.

Dismounting, he tied Four Winds to a small shrub close by. Lying down on the grass, he looked up at the marshmallow clouds softly wafting in the mild breeze. He realized that his heart was overflowing with thankfulness and gratitude to God, and to the family that raised him, and to the family that embraced him now!

At two years old, Dante had lost his parents, Nicolas and Merrin Castrinni, in a fatal car accident. He had come to live with Uncle David and Aunt Felicity Carrington, who was his mother's only sister, and his younger cousin, Olivia, who was just three months old. She was his Baby Livvy, as he called her.

He thought he could vaguely remember when Uncle David and Aunt Felicity had come to the hospital in Sudbury, where he had been taken after the accident. Then they all flew on a big airplane back to the farm. They became a close little family: Uncle David, Aunt Felicity, Olivia, and Dante. He was as much a part of this family as if he had been born into it. He belonged with them.

He had loved the farm. He could run anywhere as fast as he wanted. He had a little wagon, that he carefully pulled Olivia in. The two cousins got along well. Always very sweet, Dante was considerate of those around him. Nothing was better than Dante and Olivia sitting together on Uncle David's lap, as he read them stories.

Aunt Felicity had often told him about his father Nicholas and his mother Merrin. She would recall the wonderful trip he and his parents had made to the farm, back in 1942. She would tell him of all the lovely times they had shared together while they were there, watching baseball games, riding the old workhorse Fan, and singing around the piano while Nicholas, his father, had played the violin. They had made ice cream with an old fashioned wooden ice cream maker, and ice. Dante had even tried to crank the handle. It was too hard for him… but he could certainly manage to eat the ice cream!

Uncle David and Aunt Felicity had told Dante how his father loved to cook Italian food. His father had played violin in Toronto's Symphony Orchestra. As a baby, he and his parents had flown on another big plane to Italy to meet Nicholas' family. Although he didn't remember the plane ride, he somehow recalled being held by a great many people.

He had constantly asked Aunt Felicity about his mother. What did she look like? Aunt Felicity had told him she was beautiful. There were pictures of Dante and his parents taken at the farm that fall. She was beautiful!

For some reason, Dante had not asked about his family in Italy, and for some reason, Felicity hadn't pushed the issue. Throughout his youth he had been well aware that his Italian family was over there, somewhere! Thinking about it now, Dante was sure that his life had always been part of God's plan, and that everything had happened the way it was supposed to. He remembered when Uncle David had brought home the German shepherd puppy. Dante had named him Ben. That was the name of his favourite teddy bear.

With he and Olivia so close in age, she had followed Dante in everything he did. They had grown up the best of friends. He laughed as he remembered the experience of not feeding old Fan his oats at lunchtime, because he was busy playing ball. He was so thankful for the support of his Uncle David in driving him to Moose Jaw for ball practice throughout high school. He had great memories of the past, and was already experiencing great memories here in Italy.

CHAPTER ONE

GETTING STARTED

DAVID STILL MARVELLED AT GOD'S HAND IN MEETING AND MARrying Felicity Myra Towers…the most beautiful woman he had ever set eyes upon. She had long platinum blonde curly hair, and the bluest eyes you could ever imagine. It was no surprise that Felicity Towers won the local 4H beauty pageant every year! That wasn't just David's idea; everyone said so, and not just that Felicity Towers was beautiful, but that she was lovely in every way. She was interested in people, and to know her, as the old adage says, "was to love her". God had a wonderful plan, and David was grateful for that. He had met Felicity while he was studying agriculture at the University of Saskatoon. Born into a family of doctors and dentists, David had always wanted something different for his future. He wanted wide-open spaces, cattle, horses, and ranching. Owning a farm and living a rural life was his dream! Felicity had been in her third year of nursing at Providence Hospital in Moose Jaw and had come to Saskatoon with a youth group from a local church to attend a revival meeting of the well-known evangelist John Wesley

White. David Carrington was also in attendance that night. Both David and Felicity were drawn by the Spirit of God, and when an altar call was given, they both responded. David knelt at the altar, next to Felicity, and they both, unbeknownst to one another, made their peace and commitment to the Lord. God then began to unfold a plan that would see them stand side by side in marriage, in good times and in bad times, always strong together in the power of God's might! Maybe love at first sight would describe what they shared, but their bond also included their deep love and commitment to a third person!

They continued seeing each other. They talked over long distance phone calls. David came to Drinkwater to meet Felicity's parents, Henry and Grace Towers. Henry was the station master and ticket agent for the CPR Station on the Soo line. They lived at the train station, alongside the tracks.

Felicity travelled across the border for her first trip into the USA to meet David's family in Missoula, Montana. The family embraced this beautiful blonde girl who had won the heart of their youngest son David, and who also shared their love of medicine. Laura Carrington had often pondered over the motivations of her youngest son, and his insistence on studying agriculture in Saskatchewan, Canada. With great reluctance, he was, as well as their two other sons, allowed and encouraged to pursue his dreams. David's answer to that was simply, "It was God's plan for me to meet Felicity", and it seemed everyone agreed!!

They were married on a windy day in June 1936, shortly after graduation, in Moose Jaw, where both of them were working in their respective fields. David worked as a researcher for Ag Rep at the PFRA, and Felicity nursed in the surgery ward of Providence Hospital. A tragic accident claiming the lives of Felicity's parents, Henry and Grace Towers, a year previous, had bequeathed Felicity and her younger sister, Merrin, with a small insurance policy and a large savings account. Two years later, David heard that a section of land was for sale in the farming community of Drinkwater, complete with most of the machinery and a big five-bedroom house. They were more than interested. Upon looking it over, it was quickly decided that this would be where they would start David's dream of farming and cattle!

David had learned a lot in taking the Ag degree at university, and soon he was implementing new ways of farming. Diversity was key! His first step was to purchase a small herd of twelve black Angus-bred calves, and later on some horses, and see what might happen. It didn't take long for them to get settled, and for Felicity to resign her position at the hospital, don a pair of pants, and work alongside her new husband. Driving truck and tractor, feeding the new baby calves they had purchased, collecting eggs from a few chickens, and planting their first garden kept a girl busy!

They were very excited as they planted their first crop of wheat. But just days after they had finished seeding, in the early part of that first spring, David woke up to the smell of smoke, and the sound of the horses whinnying. Grabbing his pants, he ran outside only to see the big machine shop where he housed the tractor, the seeder, and the gasoline barrels burned to the ground. Three forty-five steel gallon gas barrels had exploded and the tops were blown open. The sharp acrid smell came from the melted rubber tires of the old case tractor and the burnt wheat in the seeder. The fire, by this time, was still smouldering, and had nearly burned out! After surveying the chaos, David hurried to the nearby barn where he could hear the loud neighing of the two young Thoroughbred colts, Beauty and Coco, that he had recently purchased from a friend in Montana. Running to the box stall in the rear of the barn, he could see the wild alarm in their eyes.

They would have heard the explosions and they were skittish and rearing. He had a very hard time getting the sliding door of the box stall open, and when he did, both horses raced through the open barn door, ran straight to the pond, and then galloped out into the recently seeded fields. It was days before he caught them. Felicity was bewildered as she viewed the scene before her eyes. What had happened? What had caused the fire? They had slept through it all. Why hadn't they heard the gas barrels exploding? As heartbroken and distressed as David was, true to his faith, he quietly put his arms around his young wife and began to thank the Lord, who had protected them from harm. Felicity shared her husband's gratitude in the midst of disaster. For if they had woken up, who knows to what lengths they would have gone to fight the fire and protect their machinery, while putting their lives in danger.

It didn't take long for their closest neighbours to see the smoke, and identify where it came from. In no time, they had arrived to help David with the cleanup. The women brought coffee, sandwiches, and pies, and everyone had a part in cleaning up. Felicity took it the hardest, and wondered if farming was the right choice for them, but David assured her he was not quitting; he would trust God to help him get back on his feet! Later that evening, one of the neighbours came over to the farm and handed David an envelope. It contained a few fifty-dollar bills, several twenty-dollar bills, some ten- and five-dollar bills, and quite a few one-dollar bills. In total, just over six hundred dollars had been collected from their neighbours to go towards a new tractor, they said. It was extremely humbling for the Carringtons to receive such a gift, but it was circumstances such as these that drew small communities and people together. Their neighbours' generosity had a deep effect on the young couple. It wasn't as though they were destitute — Felicity had her inheritance — but it signified the generosity of others, and God's hand of providence, in times such as these. They felt grateful and encouraged, as they looked forward to their first harvest together!

CHAPTER TWO

SURPRISE ARRIVAL

FELICITY LOOKED OUT OVER THE FIELD AND SPOTTED HER HUSBAND on the tractor, just a mile or so down the dirt road. She would wait till he got to the corner, then set out the supper meal on the little square card table. Pots and pans were wrapped up in old newspapers to keep them warm, and plates and utensils, salt and pepper, and butter in little packets were at the ready. Harvest was a busy time, and Felicity carried her share of the load. As David pulled up and stopped, Felicity began to set up the little table, covering it with an embroidered cloth. David swung down from the tractor and smiled at his wife. It always amused him that Felicity took the time to bring a tablecloth to the field, but in a way, he appreciated her thoughtfulness. Mashed potatoes, creamed corn, fried chicken, pickled beets; all were laid out as a feast before them. Felicity unfolded the two chairs as David bowed his head and gave thanks to the Lord for the meal, and for his wife of almost six years, and for the crop they were harvesting.

After a few bites, David wondered why his wife wasn't eating. Looking up over his cup of coffee, he saw a grimace of pain shoot across Felicity's face and eyes. Suddenly she grabbed at her back, nearly doubling over. He asked what was wrong, but she quickly dismissed it. Shortly after, another grimace covered her face and Felicity looked quite alarmed. "What is it, Fel?" he asked, using his favourite nickname for her while concern showed on his handsome face.

"Nothing, Hon," she answered, but her words didn't hold any conviction.

Turning around to get up, David noticed her eyes were wide and questioning. It seemed the pain was resonating in her lower back. "Did you fall or twist anything, Fel?" he asked.

"Not that I can recall," was her answer. Looking at her, David realized that tears had filled up the big blue eyes, and he was aware his wife was struggling to keep calm while she experienced pain. He had never seen Felicity in any so-called weakened state, and it shocked him. David put his arm around her, and directed her to the Ford half-ton she had driven to the field. Felicity tried to assure him she would be alright, and this would pass. It was just back pain; she'd had it before, though admittedly never this intense. She thought she should go back to the house and rest a bit and maybe take a couple of Aspirins. David quickly put the remainder of the meal and the dishes into the box, which he placed in the back of the truck. He helped her into the passenger side as she doubled over in pain.

Again, she expressed that she could handle it, saying, "Just let me go in and lie down", but David had other ideas. To her chagrin, he drove through the yard without stopping and headed straight onto the grid road, towards town. She actually raised her voice in alarm, and cried, "David, what are you doing?"

He answered, "Sorry, but we are going to the hospital in Moose Jaw to check this out." He had grown up in a doctor's home, and something told him that this pain was "of the serious kind".

Felicity scoffed and said there was "no need for this; just let me go lie down for a while. I'll be alright."

"You might be right," David replied, "but I want a doctor to see you. This came out of the blue, and we need to find out what is wrong." He knew Felicity was a strong girl, and with the daily work she helped him with, such as heavy lifting and lugging bales, she could very well have pulled a muscle, or maybe sprained a disc or something. He felt unsettled and helpless, and he wouldn't be persuaded to turn around and just let her rest at home.

She grumbled all the way to Moose Jaw, wanting him to turn around, and then another pain would grip her, and she would bite her tongue and moan quietly. As soon as the pain passed, she would begin explaining to David why this was a wasted trip. If she were going anywhere she should go downtown to the clinic where she might be lucky enough to be seen by her own family physician, Dr. Milton Young. He had delivered both her and Merrin, and she felt quite comfortable with him.

She insisted on not going to the emergency ward this afternoon. Felicity had previously worked on surgery, but had, on occasion, put in some shifts in the emergency ward. She knew they were always busy and that many patients frequently visited the ER instead of going to their own family doctor. "It's for emergencies," she wailed to David. The emergency unit was a busy place, and she didn't feel this was an emergency. He paid no attention. When he got to the city, he drove straight up to Lillooet Street and turned into Providence Hospital, driving around to the emergency entrance at the back. She wished she hadn't let David see her reaction to the pain, but she had, and as a result of that, she was probably on her way to a long afternoon in the ER which would probably include an X-ray or some such test. She had some Aspirin at home, and she wished she had just taken that instead of going to the hospital with a silly back pain. What she really needed was rest.

By the time David was parking at the back of the hospital, Felicity was bent over again in agony and holding back the tears. David ran in the emergency doors and soon came out with Felicity's girlfriend, RN Jenny Arnold, and Dr. Mike Lowden, who was just leaving after seeing one of his patients. Felicity had worked with them in the ER, and knew them both well. Mike joined Jenny as she ran out to the truck pushing a wheelchair.

Evaluating the situation quickly, Jenny opted to run back inside, and with the help of another nurse, she brought out a stretcher to take Felicity inside the hospital. All this time Felicity kept trying to explain she should have stayed at home… and not bothered them! David filled out some forms and tried to answer the few questions asked by the admitting nurse. His eyes were glued to the examining room they had wheeled Felicity into. One of the nurses tried escorting David out to the main waiting room, but he had no intentions of leaving Felicity, and so he stubbornly remained standing as near to the nurses' station as possible in order to listen to what might be going on behind the closed doors. A nurse left the room, running past David with a worried look on her face. She soon returned with what looked like a large clear plastic box, on a small gurney. One of the nurses at the desk looked up at David with a perplexed look on her face, but no words were spoken. David again asked, "Can I see her?" and was curtly told that he could not. He would have to wait till Dr. Lowden had examined her and assessed her condition. It seemed quiet in the ER. One of the nurses brought David a cup of black coffee. She also carried a clipboard with a paper form attached. She began asking David the questions on the chart when suddenly a shrill cry — an unmistakable shrill cry, an easily recognizable shrill cry — was heard. The cry of a newborn baby filled the quiet emergency room. No one could mistake that cry, not even David, but he couldn't seem to identify which room it was coming from, and nevertheless, it didn't really matter; he had Felicity to worry about. He did notice the two nurses at the station had whimsical smiles on their faces. Seconds later, a smiling Jenny Arnold opened the door and motioned for David to come in. He could hear the sound of a baby crying loudly, and if he was not mistaken, was that Felicity and the nurses and Mike Lowden laughing also? He hesitated, and cautiously moved in the direction of the open door. Glancing in quickly, he was overcome with emotion, and he quietly fainted! Mike managed to get David into a prone position and seated close to Felicity, who was beaming, tears running down her cheeks, holding a small bundle wrapped in a pink flannelette blanket. They were all talking at once! Five pounds, seventeen inches long, and perfect as far as they could see. She had ten toes and ten fingers, large blue eyes, quite a lot of curly light blonde hair like Felicity's, and a strong chin just like her daddy's. David was amazed at what he saw before him. Beautiful wasn't the word he would use to describe the pink bundle, or Felicity, who had just given birth! Incredible seemed to fit better! He had always thought of his wife as beautiful, but never as he saw her today. She was absolutely radiant!

He hardly had time to bend down and kiss Felicity and murmur a few words in her ear, when things began to move at a fast pace. Felicity and the baby were transferred up to the maternity ward, leaving David following behind. He was then directed to sit in another waiting room while attending nurses took over settling mother and baby.

David's head was spinning! I mean, this wasn't exactly how they had planned bringing a baby into the world, not as a surprise like this. You were supposed to find out the news, keep it a secret for a couple of months, maybe have morning sickness, pick out names and prepare a nursery, and then wait and wonder what it would be. Following this, the labour and the delivery. What happened???

"Who knows?" he said to himself, but what more could he ask for? "Are they both really alright, Lord?" David loved and believed God. He believed that every good thing came from His Heavenly Father! He had been given Felicity as his life partner, and now a beautiful daughter. His reaction to these gifts was to silently pray, "Thank you, Lord!"

Dr. Lowden came out and patted David on the back. "Nice going, David; great secret you kept from all of us!" He laughed. "All is well!

Everything is fine, no complications. Felicity did well; a natural birth, and a beautiful girl."

By this time David had grown thoughtful, and did have questions. Quite a few, for that matter. "I can't believe this," David thought. "Why didn't we know about this baby coming?" David and Felicity had no idea she was pregnant. He thought about Felicity. Yes, she had put on a little weight, but ever so little, and he had attributed that to the fact that she worked outside as hard as he did, and they both enjoyed the fabulous meals she served. David's main concern wasn't so much why, but that Felicity was alright. Dr. Lowden assured him that she was fine, and that she would remain in hospital for the next five or six days, just to sure everything was on track, and their baby girl would remain for a few days in an oxygen isolette, just to make sure she was gaining a little weight. Her birth weight was only five pounds, and they treated her as a preemie.

Dr. Lowden knew David was concerned, so he maneuvered him to the cafeteria, and ordered them a couple of coffees, and explained to David that this was a rare occurrence, called a Cryptic pregnancy. There was nothing to worry about; all was fine!

Finally, David was allowed to go into Felicity's room and spend some time looking through the nursery window at their new daughter. Baby Girl Carrington, her name card read. He couldn't get over it; they had a daughter. David and Felicity busily filled in the registration for Baby Carrington's birth certificate. It was decided quite mutually to call her Olivia Grace: Olivia, after David's great-grandmother; and Grace, after Felicity's deceased mother.

He realized he needed to phone his parents, and wondered what their reaction would be. What would the family of physicians think when they heard that David and Felicity had had no idea whatsoever that a baby was on the way? "So be it," David sighed, as he put in a long-distance call to his parents, hoping it would be his mom that answered. He was sure his brother Joe, who was in the practice of obstetrics in North Dakota, would have a laugh about this. Joe did laugh, when David called, but was pleased to hear that all was well with the new family. Joe was aware of Cryptic pregnancies, during which a woman would continue to menstruate, never suspecting she might be pregnant. He told David not to worry. It did happen! Of course, all the Missoula Carringtons were over the moon with joy, and joked that maybe it was good that David had chosen to be a farmer, and not a doctor!

The next call he placed was to Merrin Castrinni, Felicity's sister in Toronto, to share the exciting news of this new member of the family! Merrin was totally dazed at the news, and couldn't help but chuckle at the circumstances. She assured David that she, her husband Nicholas, and son Dante would be coming out to the prairies soon for a visit, and to meet the new arrival!

On the maternity ward, Felicity was treated like a queen. Because she had taken her training at Providence, both Sister Mary Cornelius (Director of Nursing) and Sister Mary Raphael fussed over both mother and baby as if they belonged to them.

David had a busy week while his wife and daughter were in the hospital. He painted the downstairs bedroom. A white crib was purchased, along with a bassinette and changing table. Jenny Arnold helped David buy flannelette and she took it home for her mother to hem into three dozen diapers. Nightgowns, undershirts, booties, Johnson's Baby Oil, Baby Soap, and cream were purchased along with safety pins and rubber pants, crib sheets, a pink satin-bound blanket, and a white knitted shawl. Felicity felt badly that she wasn't able to shop for these things herself, but David and Jenny promised her there would be lots of time for buying later! "Years of it!" David smiled.

Wrapped in the pink satin-bound blanket her daddy had bought for her, baby Olivia was taken home amidst fond farewells from two of the Sisters of Providence, and many of the staff. It was a twenty-mile drive to the farm. Both David and Felicity were glad to get home, or as Felicity said, "Get back to normal, whatever that might be." Their bedroom was awash in the late afternoon sunlight as they laid baby Olivia in her crib. Felicity was thrilled to see that along with everything else, David had purchased a beautiful oak rocking chair. Sitting down, Felicity began to reflect over the past seven days.

A baby, and she hadn't even been aware of her impending arrival! Thinking about it, Felicity couldn't help feeling embarrassment at not realizing she was pregnant. What would people think, with her not knowing she was carrying a life inside of her? She totally berated herself, while David, on the other hand, thought it was great! God had heard, and sent them a bundle from heaven. She decided that many surprises would be part of raising Olivia, along with whatever life had to offer!

That evening they received a long-distance call from her sister Merrin, in Toronto, inquiring how they were doing. It was arranged (mostly by Merrin) that she and her husband Nicholas and their two-year-old son Dante would drive out to Saskatchewan in October to meet the new family member, and to spend a couple of weeks on the farm. "Isn't it great," Merrin said, "that Dante and Olivia will be first cousins and only two years apart?"

CHAPTER THREE

MERRIN GOES TO ITALY

MERRIN TOWERS CASTRINNI WAS TWO YEARS YOUNGER THAN Felicity, and her sister's total opposite. She was a thin, wisp of a girl with raven black hair, long legs, and a daring spirit that often produced a smile or a tantalizing grin on her face. She was always ready to challenge life, whatever it faced her with. On the other hand, Felicity was blonde, fair, somewhat curvaceous, and completely involved with people and relationships.

After graduating high school, Merrin moved to Moose Jaw and started working at the new Timothy Eaton's Store on Main Street. Within six months she was offered a job in the head office in Toronto. So talented and incredibly insightful was she, that within two months, she had landed a buying trip to Venice, Italy to purchase Murano blown glass and fine china for the new department Eaton's was opening in their Toronto store. Off she went, totally confident in her ability to recognize what the need in Canada would be. She purchased the glass and china over a period of six weeks.

On her third morning in Venice, while sitting at an outdoor coffee shop, she met a young Italian by the name of Nicholas Dante Castrinni, who had been born and raised in Florence in the Tuscany region of Italy. He recognized her Canadian accent and introduced himself as a violinist who played at the Venice Opera House. They began meeting for coffee, and she was invited to hear him play a solo one evening. That was it. By the second week, they had both confessed their passionate love for each other. Merrin could not see herself returning to Canada without Nicholas, and he could not see himself letting her go. He invited her to his family's villa in Tuscany. They travelled by train through the hills to the city of Florence. While on the train, Nicholas began telling her of his family heritage.

Michaelo Castrinni, his father, had married his childhood sweetheart, Gaetane Elena Ferrara. Marco Ferrara had given his daughter the Villa Val di Pesa for a wedding gift. They had decided to raise a few horses. There was a small olive grove, and of course, the large grape vineyard. Gaetane had come from a very wealthy family, and with her inheritance, and at her insistence, it was easy to expand, and soon they had established a flourishing wine business. The winery gave gainful employment to many people living in the area, not to overlook their own children, who, no matter the circumstances, were required to come home and take part in the grape harvest. It was a must!

Five children were born to the Castrinnis: the first son, Steophano Umberto; followed by three daughters, Bianca Carlina, Elena Marsala, and Mimi Sienna; and later another son, the youngest, Nicholas Dante Castrinni, who at three years old was playing violin.

At age seven Nicholas was being tutored by a famous violinist, Nico Ulisse, and it was realized by all that his childhood dream of playing in the symphony was well within his reach. No one minded that young Nicholas didn't have the slightest interest in the winery. They were all proud of their young musical genius! Nicholas laughed in remembrance!

Merrin didn't detect any nervousness on the part of Nicholas as he introduced her to his family, but she felt a tension while the introductions were being made. Nicholas had told her she was the first woman he had ever brought home to meet the family. It didn't take long for her intuition to prove valid. Gaetane Castrinni considered the beautiful, slim, dark-haired Canadian, and instantly decided she would not be a suitable companion, least of all a wife, for her Nicholas. It seemed the whole family shared her quick unspoken assessment. Although they were extremely courteous and polite to her, there was a coolness that did not go unnoticed by Merrin!

The opinion of the Castrinni family was such that a young girl should be at home with her parents, or in school, or in a trade suitable for a woman, not running halfway around the world, unescorted, buying glass and china for a retail business. Merrin's career was not suitable, in their estimation. But, most of all, she wasn't Italian!

After being shown to her room, Merrin felt the first twinge of ambiguity. Later, when Nicholas entered her room, he expressed that he also felt the same reservation in his family, and he was puzzled, but not concerned. He knew his parents and siblings; they would warm up to Merrin. She was beautiful and vivacious, extremely knowledgeable in her career, and had a zest for life. Mama would soon understand their love for each other, and come around, as well as the rest of the family, he assured her. But Nicholas was wrong!

Later, after Merrin had retired for the night, Nicholas was called into his father's study. The family were all there, and in no uncertain terms Gaetane Castrinni proceeded to tell her son that a romance with the Canadian girl was not to be! He listened in disbelief as his mother insisted he was young and impressionable, and needed to meet women of "his own kind", being of Italian heritage, to carry on the family line. Maybe someone to share his love and musical abilities was what he needed to look for in a "life companion", she emphasized. Nicholas again could not believe what he was hearing. Mama and Papa were not prejudiced. Many of their friends in

Florence were Americans, Canadians, or from different parts of Europe. They had never spoken of any prejudice that he could ever remember. But Mama and Papa were serious. Michaelo Castrinni said very little, but nodded his head in agreement with his wife.

In no uncertain terms they expected Nicholas to end the relationship immediately! Steophano, his oldest brother and Mimi, his youngest sister were as vocal as Mama, telling Nicholas that no woman in her right mind would be travelling in Europe alone, with all the rumours of war circulating around. Mimi, in a silly immature voice, wondered if maybe Merrin was a spy! Nicholas was shocked and angered at the utter foolishness of the remark. If he had ever had an inkling about his family's reaction, he would have never brought Merrin here. He would have never subjected her to this inquisition, behind her back. Bianca and Elena, his older sisters, said nothing. Both of them were married with families of their own, and seemed to be in agreement with their parents. He had wondered why they were home this particular weekend. Had Mama called them home to help?

Nicholas looked at his family, realizing that even Mimi, the second youngest and closest to him, was in agreement with Mama and Papa. His hurt quickly turned to anger, and he told them that he and Merrin would be gone in the morning. He was sorry he had brought her home, and sorry that his family weren't going to get the chance to get to know her. Papa stood up suddenly, and began to tell Nicholas how they had given in to his desire to be a musician. How they had all sacrificed for him. They had expected all of their children to be part of the family business, but realizing his talent, had done everything to see that he had the best teachers and training money could buy.

He was allowed to leave home at an early age and study at the conservatory in Venice. Steophano and even the girls had worked hard in the winery, but Nicholas was allowed to follow his dream, so Papa said. Didn't he owe them anything?

Nicholas told his family in very clear Italian:

"Sono un musicista." (I am a musician.)
"Sarò sempre un musicista." (I will always be a musician.)
"Io odio la cantna aziendale.......non lavorerò mai in questo business." (I hate the winery business.)
"Arrivederci." (Good evening.)

That was it! Nicholas stormed out of the study and up the stairs, knocking loudly on Merrin's door. She was still awake, and Nicholas told her of his argument with his parents. He suggested they leave immediately and take the train back to Venice, but because they would need a ride to the train station, they decided they would leave early in the morning. Merrin slept little that night, and sure enough, at 6:30 a.m., Nicholas knocked on her door. He had called a taxi and was ready to leave. As they were coming down the stairs, Steophano followed them out to the portico. He tried to apologize to Nicholas, explaining that Mama and Papa were getting old and set in their ways, and "Would you please forgive them?" Steophano acknowledged Merrin, and in his own way, tried to make things right. Nicholas brushed him aside, trying to ignore him. Putting his protective arms around the astounded Merrin, he directed her into the waiting taxi. She was lost in a world of her own personal pain.

Never having met Europeans, let alone Italians, or anyone for that matter from outside of her beloved Canada, the fact that this family had judged her before they knew her was deeply disturbing to her. Shocked and bewildered by the whole situation, the two of them rode in silence back to the city of Florence.

Nicholas professed his love for Merrin, assuring her that somehow, some way, they would be together. One week before Merrin was to leave for Canada, Nicholas approached her with his plan. He had spoken to his orchestra conductor, who had called an associate of his in Toronto, who was willing to audition Nicholas with the Toronto Symphony, if he were to come to Toronto.

"Are you sure this is what you want to do, Nicholas, or are you just running from this unbearable situation?" Merrin asked. He assured her that he loved her, he had always wanted to travel to the

U.S. and Canada, and this was the perfect opportunity. And so, his decision was made. He left word with his sister Elena, and when Merrin boarded the BOAC aircraft on a bright January morning, he was at her side.

Upon arriving in Toronto, he immediately auditioned with the Toronto Symphony and was accepted on the spot. Within the next few days, he formally proposed to Merrin, she accepted, and they were married six weeks later on April 10, 1939. Nicholas was on cloud nine. He loved Merrin; he loved Toronto and his first Canadian blizzard; he loved the symphony and his new life! Soon they were able to move to a large apartment overlooking Young Street, close to where Merrin worked. Nicholas, who considered himself somewhat of a gourmet cook, enjoyed doing most of the cooking which included ravioli, lasagna, polenta, and pasta e faggioli, along with his famous Italian pizza. Every day was bliss. Adding to their pleasure, Merrin became pregnant, and close to their one-year anniversary gave birth to their son, on April 5th, 1940. David and Felicity were thrilled for Merrin, and although they had not had the privilege of meeting her husband Nicholas, they had talked to both of them on previous occasions via telephone. Now they listened intently as Nicholas shared the excitement over the birth of this little boy, who they were going to call Dante. He told them what a trooper Merrin was, and that all was well with the Castrinni family.

When Nicholas first set eyes on his beautiful dark-haired baby boy, he inexplicably longed for his family to see the child. That old adage of "Blood is thicker than water" seemed to be true. After talking to his mother on the phone several times, and hearing her desire to see the baby, Merrin consented to travel again to Italy, for a week's holiday, so his son's grandparents, aunties, and uncles in Italy could meet the new arrival.

This trip was an improvement to the first trip; apologies were not made, but the excitement and pride of little Dante's arrival seemed to overrule the feelings of hurt and unforgiveness they all seemed to carry in their hearts.

The family was cordial upon their arrival, wrapping their arms around the young father and son. Merrin was greeted with a smile, but still held at arm's length. She didn't care. After all, she thought, she would only be here for a week, so she would just relax and let bygones be bygones! She would be returning to Toronto and a long life with the two people she most loved! The family continued to speak Italian in front of her, except of course, Steophano, who spoke nearly perfect English, and who acknowledged his sister-in-law every chance he got! She knew that her mother-in-law and the girls would be busy every day cooking, and the week would be filled with family and friends visiting, eating, drinking wine, laughing, and singing every night outside on the tiled courtyard. Both Nicholas and Merrin knew that the relationship wasn't as they would have liked it to be, but they both felt they didn't want to address the unspoken distance at this time.

The Castrinnis were jubilant with this small dark-haired grandson and nephew. Dante was their delight! The first grandson! The married Castrinni daughters, Bianca and Elena, had given birth to three daughters between them. Of course they were loved, but Dante was the first and only grandson born into the Castrinni family. He was, they all admitted proudly, the image of Nicholas, and one hundred percent Castrinni. Between Grandma Gaetane, his two aunties, and three little girl cousins, someone was always carrying Baby Dante around. All three little gilrls stood in line to feed him his bottle. Grandma Gaetane went to the store room and brought out the old wooden high chair each of her children had used. After cleaning it up, and with blankets stuffed around him to keep him sitting up, they took pictures with a Polaroid camera.

So many gifts had been purchased for young Dante, it was just like Christmas! Grandma Gaetane presented the baby with the deed to a small villa that had been in her family for many years. It was known as the Villa Val di Pesa, just a thirty-minute drive from their home in Florence. Nicholas was delighted, but did hesitate at the enormity and value of the gift. It seemed that all the family were in agreement that the Villa would belong to Dante, and until his legal age, Nicholas would hold the deed in trust for his son.

Everyone reminisced fondly, remembering past holidays and weekends spent at the Villa when they were young children. They talked of hot summers when school was out, lounging around the swimming pool, sitting around the huge fire pit in the evenings, and riding horses. Aunties, uncles, cousins, and distant relatives would come for uninvited, lengthy visits. For Nicholas, Val di Pesa contained nothing but enchanting childhood memories.

Merrin felt uncomfortable about the gift, but what did it matter? They would soon be far away in Canada, and the family were here in Italy. Merrin knew his parents had expressed to Nicholas that they would never travel to Canada. They were both getting on in age, and quite comfortable where they were. Under the circumstances, that was quite alright with her. The week was quickly over, and parents and son were soon boarding the plane back home to Toronto where life would flow back into its usual routine.

CHAPTER FOUR

MERRIN'S VISIT TO SASKATCHEWAN

EAGER WASN'T THE WORD FOR WHAT FELICITY FELT, KNOWING that Merrin and her family would be arriving in a few short days. She was excited and looking forward to meeting her brother-in-law and her nephew, and the anticipation of them spending two weeks on the farm was thrilling!

She had missed her sister, and often thought about the sudden and tragic death of their parents. She remembered coming home from Saskatoon after making her commitment to Christ. Mom and Dad were the first ones she had shared her newfound faith with. Henry Towers was a bit alarmed at Felicity's news. They had always attended the United Church in Drinkwater, and her father could see no need for his daughter to be "needing any other kind of religion! And don't be bringing it up to me again," he warned.

But Grace, her mother, had a different attitude. She had smiled, and listened intently as Felicity quoted two scriptures from the Book of John, where Jesus says, "I am the way, the truth, and the life. No one comes to the Father except through Me" (John 14:6).

"I am the door. If anyone enters by Me, he will be saved, and will go in and find pasture… I have come that they may have life, and that they may have it more abundantly" (John 10:9).

"Yes, that makes it very clear," commented Grace. "I have often wondered if I was really in touch with God." Felicity had the opportunity, right then and there, to lead her mother to the Lord. Bowing her head, Grace repeated that simple prayer that had the power to reveal the Saviour and transform a life. Grace was a quiet woman, not prone to allowing emotions to rule her decisions. She prayed with sincerity, and Felicity knew that her mother had embraced the gift of Salvation through the Lord Jesus Christ!

Merrin had not been easy to share with. Just as their father had implied, she had told Felicity she didn't need a new religion, nor did she want a personal relationship with Christ, and she asked Felicity to keep her newfound faith to herself. She was on a "new adventure" in her life, and church-going was simply not on her agenda.

Since buying the farm, David and Felicity had been busy buying machinery, seed, cattle, horses, and chickens. They had spent little on the large farmhouse they lived in. They had always planned on doing this; it had just never seemed to be a priority, until now. It was decided that they would get some "new household items" before their company arrived. It was an old house, but still in good condition, and the outside had been recently painted with green trim around the many windows. The back door opened onto a small covered porch, where outdoor clothing hung on hooks on the right-hand wall. To the left, on the floor was a heavy trapdoor with wooden stairs leading down to a dark and damp dirt basement. The door was weighted down with a fifteen-inch piece of steel railroad track, on a heavy rope. Shelves covered the front wall. Most were filled with glass jars of peas, beans, tomatoes, beets, corn, carrots, pickles, relish of all kinds, crab-apple jelly, raspberries, saskatoons, and peaches. Bottles of homemade root beer were laid out side by side on the cool damp floor.

Moving into the house, you entered into a very large room containing a round table and chairs, a big wood and coal stove with a reservoir on the side for warm water, an ice box, a fold-out Chesterfield, and a small table with a radio and a Ray-O-Vac battery nearly as large as the radio itself. A wooden wall-mounted telephone adorned the east wall, between the two windows.

Red and white plastic curtains were hung in the windows. There were two other rooms, both opening off this main room. One had been intended as a living room, with a door leading out to a front porch. Presently it was used as a store room for their old school books, clothing they didn't wear, some furniture, and personal articles left to them from her parents' home. These were things she had never sorted out, including the piano she and Merrin had taken lessons on, and the old dining room table and china cabinet sent up from Missoula that had been David's grandmother's. The other room downstairs was their bedroom. Upstairs there were three large bedrooms. Yes, it seemed it was time to get their house in order!

They busily got started on the upstairs bedrooms. David painted and wallpapered, and Felicity made new curtains. On a previous trip to Moose Jaw, David had applied for a credit account, and with his farm as collateral, was found to be a "good candidate" for opening up a charge account at the Timothy Eaton's department store on Main Street.

Early on a Saturday morning the two of them and baby Olivia drove to Moose Jaw. Everything was purchased at Timothy Eaton's store, including a Sealy Posturepedic mattress, and a fifty-four-inch bedroom suite. For the living room they bought a wine-coloured velour Chesterfield and matching chair, another chair patterned in a floral upholstery, end tables and coffee table, two new lamps, along with a centrepiece of bright plastic flowers and candles to go on the new table. They bought new bed sheets, blankets, and three new sets of towels.

On David's advice, they had driven their huge old one-ton truck into Moose Jaw that day. When he backed up the big truck to Eaton's loading dock, late that afternoon, it was amazing: there wasn't even an inch left for their groceries. He had mentioned going out for Chinese food to their favourite place, the Exchange Café at the end of Main Street, but Felicity declined. She was anxious to get home and unload the new furniture. So that is what they did!

They were both elated at the amazing transformation of their "much empty" house. Lace curtains had been sewed for the living room. David painted a new coat of varnish on the dining room suite that had been shipped up from Montana from his parents' home, and just recently unpacked. The piano shone as Felicity polished it. She was ecstatic! She had gotten everything on her list, except for a new set of dishes and cutlery, and she knew exactly what she wanted. She had seen them that afternoon at Eaton's. With a promise from David that she could get the dishes before their company arrived, Felicity fell into bed that night tired, but so very appreciative of the day's purchases. It was her goal when Merrin arrived that she and her sister could relax and spend time visiting, sharing ideas on raising the two little ones that had recently joined their families, and doing whatever people do while on holidays.

Finally, now that the house was ready, Felicity started planning meals. After inquiring about the new "freezer lockers" that were run by a generator and advertised in Rouleau, the neighboring towns only grocery store. David decided to rent one on a monthly basis. He then butchered one of the young steers, giving them plenty of steaks, roasts, and hamburger. The meat was cut and wrapped in brown waxed paper.

Four chickens were killed, plucked, and frozen. One of the pigs was butchered and cut into roasts, chops, and ribs. Felicity purchased several bricks of Silverwood's ice cream from Johnstone Dairies in Moose Jaw to put in the new locker. Pies, buns, cookies, cakes, and fudge were made and tucked in the locker. Soon, it was hardly possible to close the lid. The huge garden she had planted would be just ready when the Castrinnis arrived the first week of October. Six cardboard carrying cartons, each holding six glass bottles of Orange Crush, Coca-Cola, and Cream Soda, were purchased and set aside. This would be the sisters' special treat. They would both remember how their dad, on a Saturday night, would walk uptown to the little drug store in Drinkwater and buy a case of pop and a brick of ice cream. Their mother would bring out four half pint Mason jars, the kind she used for canning. She would cut the brick of ice cream in four pieces, placing each piece in the bottom of a jar, and pour the sparkling, fizzy pop on top. A Coke float was her favourite. And yes, she remembered that her dad would always bring some straws home too.

Preparing for her company and looking after baby Olivia kept her busy. She was counting down the days to her sister's arrival. She spent time in prayer, asking the Lord to soften the heart of her beloved sister, and for this new family to know the Lord.

Finally, on a very hot prairie day, they drove up in their brand new 1942 "Candy Red" Studebaker. What a reunion! Nicholas and David hit it off as if they were long-lost buddies, which delighted the sisters, as this meant they would be able to spend time with each other and the men would also be entertained. Dante, who was Aunt Felicity's pride and joy, was enthralled with Baby Livvy, as he called her. The six of them settled in to just enjoy each other for the next two weeks.

Days were filled with David and Nicholas doing odd jobs around the farm and out in the field. In the evenings they would drive down to Wilcox to see the Notre Dame Hounds play ball, or into Moose Jaw to watch the Moose Jaw Mallards. The sisters took it easy and enjoyed sitting on the wraparound porch, drinking coffee or lemonade, sharing memories of their childhood days, and looking after Dante and Olivia.

Nights would find them playing Canasta, Crokinole, or Snakes and Ladders, listening to "The Shadow" on the battery radio, making homemade fudge or even pulling taffy, and listening to Nicholas play his violin.

Felicity was so impressed with Nicholas' talent that she asked if they might invite some friends in, and "Would he play for them?"

"Of course," he consented, and Felicity began to make some phone calls to friends and neighbours to come over that evening. Many accepted the invitation, including Jack and Myrna Lambert, a couple who had recently moved to the area. Myrna, when talking to Felicity, asked if she might accompany Nicholas on Felicity's piano. Felicity explained that Nicholas played in the Toronto Symphony, and Myrna assured her that it would be just wonderful for her to play with him. Not knowing how to say no gracefully, and not knowing what kind of a pianist she might be, for the sake of not hurting Myrna's feelings, Felicity found herself accepting her offer. Felicity took Nicholas aside and tried to excuse the fact that she didn't know how to say no, and had more or less committed to having her play. Nicholas told her not to worry; he would follow the piano as best he could, not to worry!!

But the surprise was on them! Myrna turned out to be a concert pianist in her own right! After a few piano exercises and loosening of her fingers, they made an awesome duet, with Nicholas assuring Myrna that if she were in Toronto, she could probably land a spot in the symphony. She knew most of the songs Nicholas played, and for the ones that she didn't, she sat quietly on the piano bench, her face beaming in delight! At the present time she didn't even have a piano in her own home, and was just excited to be able to play again. No one was more thrilled than Myrna. As Felicity listened she felt badly that this young woman with so much talent didn't have a piano of her own to play.

The days were dwindling down, and everyone realized it would soon be time to say goodbye.

At the supper table one evening Nicholas began to share about his family in Italy, lamenting how they hadn't accepted Merrin because of "bigotry" or "prejudice", as he called it. Yes, they had been over to Italy to see the family after Dante was born, but the situation had never been resolved, and there were still deep feelings of hurt and abandonment towards the family. He shared how he didn't fit in anymore, as a result of his trouble in forgiving them or even understanding them. It was still unsettling to both of them. He marvelled how he felt so at home here with David, Felicity, and Olivia. He recognized the peace in their home, and sincere harmony between the two of them. He made a joke that it would be nice to have that peace in his home. He and Merrin were definitely in love, but their schedules were busy, and there didn't seem to be time to do all the things they felt a family needed to do. She still worked full-time at Eaton's, and Nicholas usually performed on the weekends. There didn't seem to be any time for relaxing, and they just seemed to be always rushing and never really accomplishing what needed to get done.

It was the perfect time for David to share what his life had been like before he had accepted Christ. He simply shared the Gospel of John and the story of salvation. Nicholas, who was raised Roman Catholic, recognized the personal relationship David and Felicity shared with Christ. It was not hard for Nicholas to believe in the Holy Trinity, but he had never felt close to God, and didn't know how to get close to God. As David read scripture out of his Bible, Nicholas opened his heart up to God and tears of joy began to fill his eyes. Suddenly it all became so clear and so very simple. He heard David reading... and God's Word impacted his heart.

"For there is one God and one Mediator between God and men, the Man Christ Jesus, who gave Himself a ransom for all…" (1 Timothy 2:5).

"I am the resurrection and the life, he who believes in Me, though he may die, he shall live. And whoever lives and believes in Me shall never die" (John 11:25).

"For God so loved the world that He gave His only begotten Son, that whoever believes in Him should not perish but have everlasting life" (John 3:15-16).

When David asked in a hushed voice, "Would you like to ask the Lord Jesus into your life, Nick?", Nicholas answered without hesitation,

"Absolutely."

Before they could pray the prayer, Merrin, who was sitting next to Felicity, got up and went to sit beside her husband. Motioning with her hand, she brought Dante close to her side. "We are a family," said Merrin, "and I want us to serve Christ together." David led them in a simple prayer, and young Dante closed his eyes, as he saw his parents doing.

Simple? Yes. Life-changing? Yes. No fanfare, no horns blowing; just an honest prayer of faith, and their names were recorded in the Book of Life.

They rejoiced together! Merrin shared how she remembered the change in Felicity, and even though she was not interested in "religion", as she referred to it then, she had recognized the change in their mother, and Merrin shared how she was so thrilled their mother had accepted the Lord before she died. The girls never knew if Henry had made a commitment, but they hoped he had. Rejoicing rang through the old farmhouse that night!

On the last morning, they sat at the kitchen table drinking coffee and planning when they would be able to get together again. David was helping load the suitcases in the car, when Nicholas motioned Felicity aside. Taking her hand, he placed in it a cheque written out to Myrna Lambert in the amount of five hundred dollars. He explained to her it was for Myrna to purchase a piano and pursue her love of music! Felicity was elated by her brother-in-law's generosity, and said she would be thrilled to give it to Myrna, and help her pick out a piano! He shared with Felicity how he had heard this quiet voice inside his head speak so clearly about doing this, and that he felt very sure it was the Holy Spirit speaking to him, and would Felicity agree that it was? She smiled and wrapped her arms around him and said, "Yes, that is just how God speaks, in a small, still voice."

"After the earthquake came a fire, but The Lord was not in the fire. And after the fire came a gentle whisper" (I Kings 19:12).

Felicity had made sandwiches and cookies and soon they were all at the car. The little family joined hands and prayed for the new lives that had accepted Christ. Hugs and kisses were exchanged and soon they were driving out of the yard. The house was so quiet. Felicity sat in her rocker, thanking the Lord for the wonderful time she had had with her sister, and her family, and for the miracle of Salvation!

CHAPTER FIVE

TRAGIC ACCIDENT

THIRTY-SIX HOURS LATER DAVID HEARD THE PHONE RINGING, AND wondered who would be calling so late at night. Following him downstairs, Felicity felt a strange fear settle in her heart. News at this time of night usually wasn't good. "Hello," David answered. After a pause, he said, "Yes, yes, I am", and then she heard a sob form in his throat. He answered again, "Yes, what about the little boy?" By this time, Felicity knew the news was bad. She moved in close to David. He turned to her, asking for a pencil to write down a number. She brought him a pencil and recorded the number, and David hung up the phone. He gently put his arms around Felicity, holding her tightly, and said, "This news is bad; Nicholas and Merrin are gone. They were hit by a semi just past Sudbury, Ontario. Killed instantly, the RCMP said. Dante is in the hospital there." A coldness came over Felicity... unbelieving... Merrin and Nicholas... it couldn't be. Memories of the tragic accident that killed her parents came flooding back to her!!

Tears flowed freely from both of them. Sitting nine hundred miles away in Saskatchewan, what could they do? Who would be there for Dante? They knew they must go!

Later that morning David called the hospital in Sudbury, Ontario, to be told that Dante was fine, just some minor bruises. He had been asleep in the backseat of the car. He would be ready for discharge in the next couple of days. Would someone be coming for him? David answered, "Yes." Next, they received a call from a Roger Armbruster, the Assistant Conductor for the Toronto Symphony Orchestra. He had just been informed by the Ontario Provincial Police that one of their musicians had been in a deadly accident. It was arranged that David and Felicity would fly to Toronto as soon as arrangements were made. Roger would meet them at the Toronto airport and drive them out to Sudbury, where they would pick up Dante, and then return to Toronto to the Castrinni apartment.

Heartbroken, Felicity packed a few clothes. David called Regina Airport, explaining the emergency, and was told they could fly out of Regina to Toronto at 4:40 p.m. that afternoon. Seats were booked and the sad, grieving family drove into Regina. Felicity was grateful that David was coming with her. It would be easier with him to lean on and to help with Olivia. She realized that they would be bringing her young nephew home with them and her mind raced at the decisions that would have to be made, once arriving in Toronto.

Roger met them at the airport in Toronto, where he was able to fill them in on the details. It was dark on the highway. A semi had crossed the white line into the oncoming traffic, hitting the Studebaker head-on, killing the driver and the passenger, namely Nicholas and Merrin.

Upon reaching the hospital in Sudbury, they were taken to the children's wing, where they found Dante in the corner of a crib, red-faced and crying. As Felicity reached for him, he recognized her and his little arms reached out to her. Being just two years old, he didn't understand what had happened, but he knew he was alone and Mommy and Daddy weren't anywhere to be seen. He melted into Felicity's embrace, and the world seemed better already.

On the drive to the apartment, Roger explained that because the Symphony traveled to various parts of Canada and at times to the U.S., orchestra members were required to have on file details of their family, next of kin, contact information etc., in case of emergencies. Nicholas had made provision for the future. He had acquired a lawyer, and his personal information was up-to-date, he informed them. Roger would contact the lawyer immediately.

It didn't seem right for them to be alone in the Castrinnis' apartment without Merrin and Nicholas being there. Felicity had never been in her sister's home and was surprised to see the stunning decor. Walls were painted brightly in warm russets and tawny yellows, multiple lamps brought warmth into the rooms, and there were several pieces of antique furniture, a fairly new rich brown leather couch with matching chair, and four beautiful paintings. (These are not watercolours, Felicity realized... they are originals! Probably sent over from the family in Italy, she thought.) That realization gave into another nagging thought: what about notifying the family in Italy? Felicity didn't know anything about them, except for the few details her brother-in-law had shared while at the farm. She was well aware of the details Merrin had shared in regards to both of her visits to Florence. When they approached Roger Armbruster, who had been an absolute godsend, he informed them he had immediately notified Nicholas' older brother Steophano in Florence, and was waiting to hear back from him.

Dante immediately went to his big toy box that was in the corner of the living room. He bent over, looking for something in particular, and smiled when he pulled out a white fluffy bunny. This was the first smile they had seen on his face since the tragedy, and he beamed as he tried to place it into Baby Livvy's arms. He was very fascinated with Baby Livvy!

After settling Olivia and Dante for the night, David approached Felicity who sat on the leather couch with a hot cup of tea. He wrapped his arms around her, and she sobbed gently. "Felicity," he sighed, "this is a very hard situation we are dealing with, but remember, they asked Christ into their hearts, didn't they? That means this isn't goodbye. I know there is pain, Felicity, but we will meet again... it's just for the time being. We'll see them later, right?"

Felicity nodded. In truth... that was correct, but the grief she felt in her heart was almost too much to bear. Upon thinking of it... she wondered at God's plan, and couldn't help but ask, "What if they'd left a day later? What if they hadn't come at all?"

David replied, "If they hadn't come at all, would they have committed their lives to Christ? But, they had come, and we will have those memories forever, and they made a personal commitment, which means that we will be together again. It is hard; God's plans sometimes throw us... but we need to trust Him... and prepare ourselves for making a home for Dante. He is our responsibility, isn't he?"

"Oh, yes," cried Felicity, "he is our little boy now. That is what Merrin would have wanted; I know that for sure. I am her only relative!"

Morning came quickly. David and Felicity had their hands full feeding breakfast to the two little ones and trying to soothe Dante's broken heart. He clung to Felicity, and she to him. David left to ride along with Roger to the funeral home. He brought clothes down from the apartment for Nicholas and Merrin. Felicity remained home with the children. She had just gotten them both to sleep for a nap, when the doorbell rang. She opened it to see a tall, dark man, and two very attractive dark-haired women with him, along with looked seemed like six or seven large suitcases. "May I help you?" asked Felicity.

"Come te chiame?" (What is your name?) he asked in Italian. Seeing her hesitation, he quickly spoke in English, "I'm sorry. Who might you be?"

"I am Felicity Carrington, Merrin Castrinni's sister from Saskatchewan," she replied.

"Steophano Castrinni," he replied, stretching out his hand towards her. He motioned for the two women to step forward, and introduced them by their full names. "Elena Bethino and Bianca Pacorro. Nicholas' older sisters. They do not speak English."

Both women nodded to Felicity.

"Please come in," Felicity said. "My husband and Roger Armbruster will be home any minute," she added, guiding them inside the apartment. Both women quickly scanned the room, and spoke quietly to Steophano.

He too looked around and asked Felicity, "Where is our boy?" Hearing the inflection on "our boy", Felicity's inner guard immediately shot up, and her heart began beating a little faster.

"He's sleeping," she replied.

"We wish to see him," Steophano insisted.

"I'm sorry," said Felicity, "he has been very upset and hasn't slept much since the accident, and he's just finally fallen asleep, Mr. Castrinni. I will not be waking him up, until he wakes up himself!"

"Si, si", (yes, yes) came the reply, again in Italian. Again, he turned and spoke softly to the two women, and they said nothing. Felicity could see the pain in their eyes, and realized their grief at the loss of their brother. She reached out her hand to Steophano Castrinni.

"I am so sorry for your loss, Mr. Castrinni; please convey my sympathy and condolences to your sisters for me. We just met Nicholas these past two weeks, when they spent holidays at our farm," and suddenly the tears flooded her eyes, and she was overcome with her own grief. Thankfully, at that moment David returned with Roger Armbruster. More introductions were made, and David ushered the Castrinnis into the living room and settled them down in chairs. Felicity was only too glad to escape to the kitchen and prepare coffee for the guests.

As she returned with a tray of coffee and cakes, Steophano turned and spoke quietly to both sisters, and they acknowledged Felicity with slight nods of their heads.

After a brief conversation, Roger Armbruster, who happened to speak a little Italian, was able to convey their plans to David and Felicity. He told them that the Castrinnis had planned on staying at the apartment, but since the Carringtons were already there they would not mind going to a hotel close by. Felicity looked at the family and was overcome with a deep sadness, but at the same time, a niggling fear settled over her. Roger shared with Steophano the plans that had been made prior, by his brother, and that instructions had been left at the Symphony office, in detail, for any needed arrangements. When Steophano asked for the name of Nicholas' lawyer, Roger gave it immediately.

Bianca gestured towards one of the doors and spoke to Steophano, who turned to Felicity and asked, "When do you think the boy will awake?"

Felicity, who had never been known as rude or suspicious, answered curtly, "His name is Dante, and I'm hoping he might sleep for another hour or so." David was surprised at the curtness in her voice, but said nothing. After a few more minutes of talking in hushed tones, the three of them got up, and said they would like Roger to take them to a hotel, and would it be alright if they came back in the evening to see their nephew?

"Of course," David replied, and began to help Roger carry the many suitcases to the ground floor. Her guests seemed to have left abruptly, leaving Felicity with a feeling of apprehension. Had they come just for the funeral of their beloved brother, or were there other plans in the works? Their interest in Dante was of course, natural. He was their nephew! But were their plans to take Dante back to Italy? A wave of nausea hit Felicity in the stomach and she felt faint. This couldn't be. Dante was only two years old, her only sister's child, born in Canada. If she had to fight, she would. He would be coming home with her! She cautiously opened the door to Merrin's bedroom and could almost picture her sister sitting at the dresser combing her long black hair. The room smelled faintly of roses and she recognized Merrin's perfume in the air. Lace tie-back curtains covered the big bay window, and in the corner of the room, Dante slept soundlessly in his crib, his little face still flushed from crying for Mommy and Daddy. Her heart gave a lurch! She knew in the next few days she would have to pack Dante's clothes, personal belongings, and of course, his toys, but she had no idea what they were to do with Merrin's and Nicholas' personal belongings. She supposed the lawyer would advise them of that. She cautiously opened her sister's dresser drawers... looking for what? She didn't know, and she didn't feel comfortable doing it. She closed the drawers immediately. She opened Dante's top dresser drawer, presumably to get an idea of his clothes. There, sitting on the very top, she saw his baby book. Again, she shuddered in sorrow. It was the one she had sent down when he was born. Opening it cautiously, she knew she would see pictures of Merrin and Nicholas, and she didn't know if she could get through that, but instead, on the first page was what looked to be Dante's original birth certificate. Surreptitiously, she quickly picked it up and placed it in her skirt pocket. Taking the book with her, she left the room, opened her suitcase, and placed the folded certificate inside the zippered flap. The book she placed amongst her clothing, to view at a later date. She would be the one taking the little boy home, not the family from Italy. Merrin would not have wanted that.

Later that evening the family came to see their nephew. David welcomed them and offered coffee, which they refused. Felicity had just brought Dante out of the bathtub; his cheeks were flushed from the steam and his hair was still damp and curly. She had offered him a choice of two pairs of pyjamas to wear, and smiling, he had hesitantly picked out the ones with the red airplanes on them. These were his favourite! Bianca gently approached Dante and reached her arms out to take him, but Dante quickly declined. Instead, he laid his head down on David's neck, closing his eyes. They all realized he didn't know them, but they also wanted to embrace him. He was their only nephew. The atmosphere grew tense for a minute or two, until David said they didn't want to upset him, to which they all agreed. Steophano quietly stood up and stood close to David, saying nothing. All were surprised when Dante lifted up his head and looked directly into the eyes of Steophano. Did he notice the resemblance Steophano had to his father? He looked inquisitively into his uncle's eyes, and then a very small smile touched the corners of his little mouth.

Funeral arrangements were made with the help of Michael Gallo, the lawyer Nicholas had hired since his immigration to Canada. He and Nicholas had become good friends and they played together in a late-night hockey league. At a time when the Carringtons were alone with Michael, they asked about the intentions of Steophano Castrinni in regards to Dante. Michael replied that the Castrinnis had made it very clear: they wanted to return to Italy with Dante. David assured the lawyer that it was the Carringtons who wanted to take Dante home to Saskatchewan, and raise him. David made his case very clear to the lawyer: they wanted Dante; after all, he was a Canadian citizen and only two years old, Felicity was his blood aunt, and he would have a sister in Olivia. He had spent the previous two weeks with them, at the farm. They didn't want to share Merrin's recollections about the Italian family, especially how she was treated while visiting them, on two different occasions, but it seemed Nicholas had previously shared that particular information with Michael, and he was in complete agreement with David and Felicity being made legal guardians of Dante. He was very sure the courts would favour them, as opposed to the Castrinnis. If necessary he would speak on behalf of the Carringtons.

Michael would take charge of dispensing the finances and he would be responsible for closing up the apartment after the furniture was sold. He was aware of the Villa Di Pesa, and the deed held in trust for Dante. The Castrinnis had expressed that there was nothing in the apartment they wanted, except for the four oil paintings that hung in the living room and bedrooms which had been gifts from their parents, and of course, they wanted Dante.

That evening a sobbing Felicity clung onto David's arm as they viewed the lifeless bodies of the two people they loved so dearly. Merrin was as beautiful in death as she had been in life. Her long black hair and the touch of pink lipstick made her look like a sleeping princess. Felicity had many pictures of Merrin in her mind, but she would remember her like this, almost smiling. Both she and David silently thanked the Lord that this couple had accepted Christ into their hearts. They would meet again in heaven.

The funeral service for Nicholas and Merrin was held at St. Michaels, one of the largest Roman Catholic cathedrals in downtown Toronto. It had been built in the mid-eighteen hundreds with beautiful stained-glass windows, steeples, and spires. Nicholas attended St. Michaels whenever he was not travelling outside of Toronto with the Symphony. The church was renowned for its famous boys' choir, and today, as they sung the offertory, all thoughts were centred on the sadness of this tragic loss. There was always the question, why? Symphony conductor Maestro Myron Feinstein from the Toronto Symphony spoke in warm tones about the young Italian and his beautiful wife whom he had come to know so well in just a couple of years. It was evident that Nick and Merrin were an integral part of a group of people who had an appreciation for life, music, and good values and who were devoted in their personal relationships with each other. Two or three close friends shared recollections of good times spent in the Castrinnis' home and of the young couple's delight when Dante was born. All in all, tribute was paid and mourners were left to grieve and celebrate their lives with individual memories.

Near the end of the service, Steophano Castrinni suddenly arose from his pew and walked up to the lectern. David and Felicity were instantly aware that this had not been a planned event. The Castrinnis had been present when the plans for the service were made with the Funeral Director, and at that time it had been decided that neither of the families would be speaking. Nevertheless,

Steophano waited at the side until the current speaker was finished, and then quickly took his place.

"I am Steophano Castrinni, oldest brother of our beloved Nicholas. I am here at the request of our parents, Michaelo and Gaetane Castrinni, and with the support of my two younger sisters." He proceeded to introduce his sisters to those in attendance. The two sisters arose from where they were sitting, on cue, as if they understood exactly what their brother was saying. After they had sat down again, Steophano continued, "We deeply mourn the passing of our brother. We are here to pay our respects to Nicholas' memory, and carry out his wishes, and the wishes of our parents. We will be making the necessary arrangements to take the boy back to his family in Italy, and to his appointed inheritance, as was Nicholas' desire. Thank you for coming." He then walked sombrely back to his seat. Neither David nor Felicity could believe what had just been said. In fact, Steophano's declaration seemed to bring the huge cathedral into stark quietness. No mention of Merrin! The cliché about "hearing a pin drop" was extremely evident. Steophano Castrinni had taken this opportunity to speak his intentions publicly.

Felicity and the children were sitting in the front pew on the right-hand side of the church, while the Castrinnis sat on the left. David placed Dante, who had been on his lap, close to Felicity's side, and she moved baby Olivia to her other shoulder and pulled him in close to her. He had sat wide eyed and very quiet through the long service, and she couldn't help but wonder what was going through his little mind.

David Carrington was a quiet man, but a man of deep convictions, and no one's fool. Before Steophano's foot had left the step of the dais, David was on his feet, moving forward toward the pulpit. Surprise covered the face of Father Phelan, celebrant for the service that day. He smiled at David, and with a gesture of his hand, ushered him forward to speak.

"My name is David Carrington. My wife, Felicity, is Merrin Castrinni's s older sister. Nicholas was my brother-in-law. Merrin and Nicholas had recently visited us at our home in Saskatchewan. It was during their return from our home that this accident happened. Over the past two weeks, we became good friends. It was a time of sharing our hearts and our desires in life. We shared intimate conversations concerning the mystery of life we are all called to journey. It was during one such conversation I had the opportunity to share my personal relationship to Jesus Christ. Nicholas and Merrin responded, and prayed a simple prayer, and at that time they made a personal commitment to the Lord Jesus Christ. I know this isn't a practice in all churches, but it is very clear in the scriptures that a person must be born again before he can see the Kingdom of God. There is only one mediator between God and man, and that is the man Christ Jesus. While spending time with us, Nicholas was drawn to the words in the gospels, and over the days of their visit, a deep change began to settle upon him and emerge in his attitude towards life. He desired peace and contentment in his home. Nicholas' hope was shared by our sister Merrin, whose words were, and I quote, 'We are a family, and this is what we need... to know God in a personal way. This will keep our family together.'"

At this point, the priest began to inch towards David, as if to say "Enough said", but David continued: "My wife Felicity and I feel very strongly that this child, whose name is Dante, should and will be part of our lives here in Canada. At a later date, when he is old enough to decide, he will be free to build relationships with his family in Italy. We believe this to be the wishes of Nicholas and Merrin Castrinni." As he returned to his pew and sat down, Felicity squeezed his hand proudly. She knew that David had to respond to Steophano's public outburst, even if it didn't seem the right thing to do at a funeral. Steophano Castrinni's face was dark with rage. His sisters glared at David with disdain on their faces, and Felicity wondered if maybe they did understand English after all! It seemed that this somewhat invisible struggle over the custody of young Dante Nicholas Castrinni was now out in the open.

Back at the apartment, just hours after the funeral, Steophano angrily opened up the question of Dante's future, but not before he told David in no uncertain terms how offended he was that David would dare speak publicly of anyone's need to be born again or to read the gospels. Nicholas, he said, had been raised in the Church of Rome as a dedicated Catholic, and he did not need David interfering with his faith, nor the church's doctrine, for that matter! He personally felt insulted. David made no apology, nor did he respond to this outburst. Looking to Michael Gallo, Steophano explained that it was his parents' explicit wishes for him to bring the boy back to Florence, immediately, where he would live with them. David quickly and vehemently opposed any idea of that, and Felicity said she would go to court if she had to. She also remarked that Dante had a name, that he was a person, and she couldn't understand why Steophano referred to him as "the boy". That greatly offended her! Contention and tension were running high, and it seemed as if an enormous argument would ensue. Then Michael Gallo, Nicholas' lawyer, offered a different line of reasoning in support of the Carringtons' claim in taking Dante into their home. A court hearing could be arranged, if that is what Steophano wanted to pursue, but it would take time, and paperwork, and in his estimation, the Carringtons would be the most likely choice. "After all," he said, "the child is Canadian, a blood relative to Felicity, and would be in a home where the family is young. In Olivia, there would be a younger sibling, which would be good for Dante. Also, upon going through Nicholas' papers, a birth certificate for Dante was not available. It had probably been misplaced," he said, "but to take Dante out of the country, that paper must be produced, along with proof of the court's authority." His advice to the Castrinni family was to leave Dante under the care of the Carringtons and in time cultivate a relationship with him. Of course, they were free to pursue a legal battle, but in his opinion, for the good of the child, the Carringtons would be favoured. He did not apologize for his advice, as he remembered vividly the conversation that

Nicholas had shared about the Castrinnis' treatment of his wife on the two occasions of them visiting the family in Italy. Steophano pondered this advice, and finally asked if he could consult privately with his sisters, maybe in the kitchen? They did so, and loud shrill voices could be heard. Finally, a resigned quietness was evident, and the three of them strode into the living room. Mustering up her courage and sense of hospitality, Felicity stood up and reached for Steophano's hand, but without any acknowledgement of her gesture, he brushed her aside, bowed slightly to Gallo, and tensely announced his imminent departure.

"I would like the paintings, as we agreed," he said in a detached voice. They had been taken off the wall previously, by Felicity, and were leaning against the wall by the door. They were not wrapped. Elena and Bianca wasted no time in reaching for the paintings. They picked them up, without bothering to look in the direction of the Carringtons.

"Grazie per la sue gentilezza," (Thank you for your kindness) Steophano said softly to Michael Gallo. He bowed to Felicity and David and said, "Saremo in contact a una data in retardo." (We will be in contact at a later date.) Without saying goodbye, they turned towards the door, opened it, and filed out quietly with Steophano in the lead and the two sisters in his footsteps. The three adults in the room were left at a loss for words.

Michael smiled a poignant smile, and said he was fairly certain this would not be the last time the Castrinnis would clash over the matter of taking Dante back to Italy. He could see anger and determination in their quest to meet their parents' wishes, as they had said. He would work on preparing the paperwork which would name the Carringtons as legal guardians for Dante. In the meantime, he gave the Carringtons permission to return with Dante to their home in Saskatchewan, and he would settle up all the details. If Felicity wanted to take anything, anything at all from the apartment, now would be the time to do that, as he would be arranging the closure of their possessions. He would be getting all the finances in order, into a trust for Dante. He bid them goodnight, and said he would call in the morning.

Felicity reached out to Michael and asked him to wait a minute. She went into the bedroom and came out with Dante's baby book and his birth certificate. Her cheeks were red and she couldn't control her tears. As she handed the birth certificate to Michael, she said, "I'm sorry. I can't explain why I took it." She had been impetuous and scared. She looked over at David, and broke into uncontrollable sobs. David pulled her sobbing body close, cradling her in his arms.

Michael had been very much aware of Merrin's treatment on her first visit to the Castrinni family. He put a comforting arm on Felicity's shoulder, and said, "Don't worry, Felicity. This is how it should be. Dante needs a family. We'll deal with the Castrinni family, if and when the time comes. Please don't worry!" Michael bade them goodbye, and left the apartment.

David and Felicity were shaken at the turn of events, and the animosity directed towards them. "Where do we go from here?" Felicity asked David.

"We need to be getting home soon," replied David. "Let's put this behind us for now, and decide what we want to take home for Dante. Gather up anything you feel he would want as remembrance of his parents, and anything you would like of your sister's." David suggested, "We can have items shipped to Moose Jaw, to be kept in storage for Dante."

"Yes," thought Felicity, "Dante needs some things to link him to his parents."

A walk through the apartment found them setting aside such items as Nicholas' cherished violin, sheet music and a music stand, a box of trophies he had attained in his young career as a violinist, family pictures, passports, rings, Merrin's diary, and of course she had the baby book in her possession already! Her eyes lingered on the antique porcelain bedroom lamp, which had been given to Merrin and Nicholas, by them, as a wedding gift. Tearfully, Felicity said she would like to take it home with her. They would take Dante's crib, and all of his toys. They would take a twin bedroom suite from the storage room that must have been purchased for Dante to use when he got a little older. They would take a large vintage roll top desk from the foyer. It seemed to be an essential part of the big room's decor. David thought Dante might like to have that, especially when he grew older. Everything was set aside to be shipped by train to Moose Jaw, and out to Drinkwater. Arrangements were then made for the flight home, and for Felicity and David, it couldn't happen too soon.

A few weeks after returning home from Toronto, David went into town for the mail. Mrs. Wilma Price, the postmistress, was quite excited as she handed David a long blue linen envelope stamped from Italy. Driving home, David wondered what developments regarding Dante would be inside. The letter was addressed to Mr. Dante Castrinni, in care of Mr. and Mrs. David Carrington.

Felicity's hands shook, but she didn't hesitate as she opened the long blue envelope. Inside, folded on a matching piece of blue stationery, was a money order for fifty dollars in Canadian funds, with a terse note scrawled on the bottom,

"For the needs of the boy."

She definitely knew the sender was Steophano, who was still referring to his nephew as "the boy". It wasn't so much anger that rolled over her; it was that old blanket of fear. What were they up to? What was the reason behind the money? What were they supposed to do? Should they return it? She asked David, who replied, "Definitely not. This money is for Dante, and for Dante it shall be. I'll call Michael Gallo and make sure we do things properly. I'm sure if we open up another account separate from the one he already has, it will be alright. We also need to talk to Michael about the legal papers giving us permanent custody of Dante."

The Toronto lawyer assured them that it would be fine to open up another account for Dante. He had not received any correspondence in any form from the family in Italy. He quickly assured them that the papers were on their way to Saskatchewan, giving the Carringtons legal custody over their nephew.

Felicity had no problem putting the money away for Dante, but she still had to deal with the uncertainty of the reason behind it. The following month they received another money order, this time for thirty-five dollars, which they deposited in Dante's newly opened account at the Royal Dominion Bank. The following month a money order for fifty dollars arrived, and every month after that, without fail. Most often it was for fifty dollars, sometimes a little less, but never less than thirty-five dollars. On occasions such as Christmas and the month of his birthday, it would be for one hundred or two hundred dollars. The money orders were always in the same blue linen envelopes. There was never any inquiry of how Dante was doing. No news or questions from his grandparents or cousins. Just the money orders. They arrived as regularly as clockwork, and just as regularly, they were deposited in the bank in Moose Jaw. This money was never touched. It would all be Dante's one day. The Carringtons looked upon Dante as "our son".

CHAPTER SIX

THE AKIRA FAMILY

ONE SUNDAY AFTERNOON, DAVID STOPPED AT THE DRUG STORE and confectioners' shop in town to get some Coca Cola. While inside he noticed a family consisting of a mom, a dad, and two little girls. The couple seemed friendly and a conversation commenced. Their names were Kenshin and Eiko Akira, and the small twin girls, Ami and Mai, were just three years old. They had come to Moose Jaw six months ago from Vancouver B.C. after spending seven months in the internment camp at Hastings Park Racecourse. The twins had been born in the camp. After the bombing of Pearl Harbor, in 1942 Japanese Canadians were given twenty-four hours to pack their belongings before being interned. Their land, businesses, and other assets were confiscated by the government and sold, and the proceeds were used to pay for their internment. In 1945, the government extended the Order in Council to force the Japanese Canadians to either go to Japan and lose their Canadian citizenship, or move to eastern Canada. The Akiras came to Moose Jaw, Saskatchewan in 1948.

Kenshin's maternal uncle, Naoko Yoritomo, owned and operated the fruit and vegetable store on Main Street, in Moose Jaw, and he offered his nephew a job there. Kenshin was grateful for the opportunity to work. The family had bought a second-hand car, and every Sunday afternoon Kenshin took Eiko and the little girls for a drive outside the city. This enabled them to explore their new surroundings. One day they stopped in the small town of Drinkwater, eighteen miles east of Moose Jaw. It was in the local drug store they met David Carrington. After a few minutes of introduction, David invited them out to the farm, which was only three miles from town. When they arrived, they admired and marvelled at the big house, the machinery, the huge garden, and the farm animals.

Kenshin had never been on a wheat farm before, and he found himself amazed at the big red Cockshot combine and swather David drove. Eiko, on the other hand was mesmerized by the size of the vegetable and flower garden that Felicity had planted. Longing shone in their eyes at the wide-open spaces of the prairies. Kenshin asked David if he would ever need help on the farm, and David replied that in the summer, they were always in need of drivers for the grain truck and combine. Kenshin was interested and that summer, during his two-week vacation, he came out to the farm and worked for David. Working outside on the farm, he loved the open spaces, the clean air, and the cool, crisp evenings. He even volunteered to come out and work weekends. Somehow a deep friendship was forged quickly between the two couples. Eiko, who was a few years older than Felicity, was full of solid advice and great understanding, and she was so ready to learn new Canadian ways. At first she spoke little English, but it wasn't long before she and Felicity were able to share insightful conversations. A deep sense of family developed. While working with Kenshin over the summer, David offered him a full-time job on the farm. He would provide housing for the family, and in return Kenshin would be responsible for the daily tending of the animals. This included feeding the cattle, horses, and chickens, cleaning the barn and chicken coops, and planting and tending the garden. David would concentrate solely on the planting and harvesting of the wheat, and the building up his horse and cattle herd. Agreements and arrangements were hastily made. Eiko's head was full of excited plans for what they would do with the large garden. This was to be a full-time arrangement. David knew he had to have a warm place for them to move into in the fall, so he and a neighbour worked together and transformed the big stationary granary into a comfortable home for the Akiras.

The main part of the house consisted of a large room with a kitchen on one end and living room on the other. After cleaning it out, insulating and covering the walls with new white-panelled wallboard, and adding three new windows, one of them being a large bay window for Eiko's beloved houseplants, two new bedrooms and a bathroom were built, along with a new front door. Another trip was made to Timothy Eaton's, this time by David and Kenshin. David purchased a kitchen stove with a side reservoir for water, linoleum for the entire house, a small bank of mahogany kitchen cupboards, white Arborite countertops, and a stainless-steel sink. Kenshin proudly purchased a Singer treadle sewing machine for Eiko. The Akiras would be moving in on the last day of August, so David and Felicity rushed to get things done.

It was wonderful having them on the farm. Kenshin enjoyed his work, and was always in a good mood. He was so polite and courteous. He knew that David Carrington was a good man, and one he was proud to work for. The two families often found themselves eating supper together. Eiko was, of course, a first-rate Japanese cook, and she loved cooking. The Carringtons learned to appreciate katsudon, or deep-fried pork cutlet, served with a sweet sauce over rice; meshimono, a rice mixture with chicken and vegetables; and mochi, or sweet rice cakes; followed by steaming hot green tea, "Shizuoka" brand, if it was available.

Green tea was always drunk out of small fine porcelain bowls, with no handles. Eiko always smiled as David struggled with his large hands trying to bring the delicate small bowl to his mouth.

49

He appreciated that the art of drinking the tea was as important as enjoying the flavour, and so he tried desperately to drink with good manners.

That winter Eiko spent time planning the garden she would plant in the spring. Felicity spent time, that same winter, thanking the Lord that she wouldn't have to plant the garden in the spring! Maybe Eiko would even enjoy helping with the canning, she hoped, a job she always did faithfully, but didn't really enjoy.

The children grew and fully enjoyed one another! Things were going well on the Carrington farm!

One spring morning Felicity got up early and left the farm before eight o'clock, driving the Ford half-ton truck. She told the children to wait for a surprise. Upon arriving home, she called Kenshin to help her unload the truck. He smiled as he carried four large cardboard boxes into the house, lying them gently on the kitchen floor by the stove. The boxes were about thirty-six by thirty-six inches square and about ten inches high. Perforated holes surrounded the sides and tops of the boxes. Each box contained twenty-five small yellow baby chicks, and if you put your head down to the holes, you could hear the cheep, cheep, cheep of baby chickens, but you couldn't see them. The children were instructed not to open the boxes. Kenshin and Felicity would go out to the new chicken house and light the brooder stove, after which they would return for the boxes. Olivia and the twins lay on the floor, trying to peek into the ventilation holes in the sides of the boxes, but unfortunately, they couldn't really see inside very well. The twins had never seen a baby chicken before, so Olivia said, "I will get one out to show you! Just one!" She carefully opened one corner of a box, and gingerly reached her hand in. She removed one small, soft, yellow chick and handed it to Ami.

Seeing this, Mai cried, "Livvy, me one please!"

Again, Olivia reached into the box, and handed Mai a small yellow bird. All three of them sat admiring the tiny little yellow balls of fluff! Suddenly Ami screamed in a high voice, "Look!" Around the room, running from here to there, were twenty-three yellow balls of fluff, skittering every which way! Into the living room, out onto the front porch, under the Chesterfield and chairs, and all over! Quickly the little girls began picking up the little birds, trying desperately to get them back into the box. But by the time they got their hands in and out of the box, another chick would hop out and run. Olivia knew they needed help, but dreaded calling her mother. Thankfully it was Kenshin who returned to the house, and he couldn't help but be amused at the sight of his two little girls with chicks in their hands. Mai had even tried to put one into her dress pocket. He helped the little girls round them all up, and Felicity, if she ever knew, didn't ask as to why it took them so long to bring the babies out to the brooder.

CHAPTER SEVEN

IN REGARDS TO THE CHILDREN

Raising two children kept David and Felicity busy, but they loved every minute of it. Dante had settled in well, and was genuinely fond and attracted to his "Baby Livvy", as he called her. He adored Uncle David, and spent time sitting on his knee, reading stories of farm animals and playing with the little puppy that the family had acquired. When the eight-week-old German shepherd was brought home, Dante was allowed to name him. He came up with the name of Gentle Ben, so Ben it was! The dog proved to be the delight of all of the family. He was a beauty. Not a big dog, he was a little on the slight side with beautiful silver and black markings. He was smart, but very timid, and for the first few days he hid from every noise and cowered in the corners so as not to be seen. David was concerned that Ben had been mistreated, and wondered if he would ever come around to trusting them. But within a few days of being cajoled and talked quietly to, the puppy made friends. Though he attached himself primarily to Felicity, he was loved and adored by all.

Work progressed on the farm with seeding, harvest, farm chores, and every day much the same, but there was never a dull moment. Wintertime found them entertaining friends, planning games in the evenings, and hosting a small Bible study. Deep friendships were formed in the small village of Drinkwater. Every week Myrna Lambert and her husband insisted on bringing over a surprise dessert for everyone. Coffee and juice were provided by Felicity, and conversation centred on God and His infinite plan for mankind. Myrna would play the piano and they would all gather round singing. She played many of the old time big band songs as well as praise songs to the Lord! Members of the Bible study were aware of Dante's father giving Myrna the money to purchase her own piano. Myrna's music brought fond tears to the eyes of David and Felicity.

Felicity was an avid reader, and so trips to the Moose Jaw Library were part of her monthly ritual. She was constantly journaling and jotting down family situations and memories, hoping to one day write and record them in a book that she would probably finish years later!

The spring of 1949 brought great excitement and anticipation to everyone in the surrounding community, because electricity was coming to Saskatchewan! Soon the power poles were up and the house and barn were wired. Felicity had dreams of a buying a new refrigerator, washing machine, and electric iron. Until now, an ice box with ice in the top was all they had to keep everything cool. Washing clothes was a big job, and ironing was done with flat irons kept hot on the coal and wood stove, so on a hot day, if you had to iron, it wasn't her most enjoyable task! And packing away the gas and coal oil lamps was a colossal moment for both David and Felicity! A trip was again made to Eaton's in Moose Jaw with the big truck, this time to purchase a fourteen-cubic foot Admiral refrigerator, an electric washing machine, an electric coffee percolator, a new electric iron, and an electric toaster. Felicity was enthralled with the new refrigerator. The inside of it was a pale turquoise blue colour, with shelves of stainless steel and clear glass.

On the side door was a row of indentations, in which you could place eighteen eggs. Above the egg shelf was a clear plastic lift-up lid for butter and cheese. Before David had the cardboard wrapping off the fridge, Felicity was out in the hen house gathering eggs and getting them washed so she could set them in the refrigerator. As David was hauling out the cardboard, Felicity was filling the egg shelf with eggs.

Olivia, who was small, slight, thin, and quiet, loved school, liked reading, and was very devoted to her best friend, Marlene, whose mother was the local post mistress. Marlene would often be at the farm for the weekend. She loved to join Olivia and Dante at play. Most times Dante would choose to go to the field with David, and let the girls do girl things.

Since birth, Olivia had suffered from various allergies. Her eyes were significantly affected, and school recesses would often find her inside the school doing light activities. The spring she turned nine, she went for an allergy test in Regina. Since David was seeding, Felicity had to take Olivia alone, driving their big one-ton truck. It seemed a long drive to Regina, the capital city, and finding the Medical Arts building and parking the big truck were challenging tasks, but Felicity managed! Olivia's allergy test revealed that she was allergic to animal dander, wheat, lilacs, and of all things, her own hair. What a conundrum! She lived on a wheat and cattle farm, the sidewalk to the school was lined with lilac bushes, and she had long curly hair. What would they ever do?

"First," Felicity told her, "you will be excused from any work in the barn or garden," (Hurrah for Olivia!) "and secondly, we'll have to cut your hair short." When they became aware of the problem, the school board in Drinkwater cut down most of the lilac bushes that bordered the sidewalk to the school. This did not help Olivia's popularity. She was often teased for having short hair, for having to get drops in her eyes, and for not being sports-minded! Kids could be cruel!

Drops had been prescribed for her eyes, and every day Dante was called upon to administer them at noon time, and again at the last recess. He would go with her into the school office and put a drop in each eye, a process which always caused Olivia embarrassment! Because of these restrictions, she began to enjoy the peace and quiet of her own private space, that being her large sunny upstairs bedroom. It had been wallpapered a soft butter yellow design, with white curtains. An east window gave the room plenty of light. It became her private sanctuary. Bookshelves covered a portion of one wall, and a window seat had been built under the east window. You could find her there most of the time.

David arrived home one evening with an old upright desk he had purchased for her at a local auction. It had many drawers as well as small pigeonhole slots to hold a variety of papers. Olivia was delighted. It was very similar to the desk Dante had in his room, which she had admired on many occasions! Hours were spent at this desk doing homework and writing. As a passionate amateur novelist, her first novel, entitled *The Quest for Amigo*, featured a beloved horse. Alone in her room, she loved the solitude as well as her writing.

As shy as she was, she excelled in the Regional Oratory contests between the small-town schools, and she was a member of the school's drama team. When it came to sports, she did not shine. On one occasion she had been asked by a teacher to keep score for a baseball game, but because of her lack of interest, she was usually looking away or talking when someone scored a run. Soon the job was given to another! In the late spring, when surrounding schools participated in track and field meets, she was never a part of this; she just watched from the sidelines.

One morning recess when most of the kids were practicing for the school's annual Field Day, she noticed an older boy chasing a smaller boy, who was crying. Ever the defender of the young, Olivia ran over to see if she could help. Mistake! In the hand of the older boy was a green and yellow striped garter snake. She froze on the spot. In reality, it was probably only ten inches long, but in her eyes, it was at least two to three feet long. The older boy laughed and yelled fiendishly, "Here, Olivia; you'll like him!" Bending low to the ground, he threw the snake at her. With Olivia frozen in a state of fear, the snake landed on her foot and quickly encircled itself around her ankle. She couldn't move, and she couldn't scream. Everything was in slow motion. The snake twisted tightly around her ankle. She could hear the kids on the playground laughing in the background, when suddenly, out of nowhere, Dante appeared. He grabbed Olivia by the shoulder with one hand, and grabbed "the monster" by the tail with his other hand, flinging the snake as far as he could into the nearby caragana bushes. He embraced Olivia, who by this time was hysterical. The principal was called out, and a traumatized Olivia was taken into the school office. Felicity was called to take her home for the day. All the kids were only too happy to tell Dante who had tortured Olivia with the snake. It was big Phil Bates, a renowned bully! It's probably a good thing we don't know the conversation Dante had with Phil, but suffice to say, his days of bullying and tormenting the younger kids seemed to come abruptly to an end that day on the playground. This made many of the smaller children happy and turned Dante into a hero, and not just in the eyes of his cousin! No doubt about it, Dante was Olivia's champion!

One day when Marlene was over, the girls were bored. As they wondered what to do, Felicity encouraged them to "use their imaginations", and so they did. They decided they would play telephone operator in the vacant upstairs bedrooms. With two dozen long shingle nails, some string, and a hammer, they hammered the nails into the wall and attached the string to each end of the nails. With a yellow chalk, they drew a box around them, on the wall. A chair was placed in front of the so-called "telephone board" and they took turns transferring calls all over the province! It was great fun, until Felicity saw the nails hammered in the walls, but as the girls reminded her, she had said to use their imaginations. She didn't comment, except to say that the next time they had an idea, they should check with her first!

One summer Eiko and Felicity worked on a large community project. There would be a traditional Japanese Tea Party, a penny parade, and a craft sale. They needed every minute they could spare to plan this event. So, it was decided that for the months of May and June, the children would travel the three miles to school driving a little buggy pulled by old white Fan, the retired workhorse. This was a novelty, until Dante realized he would be the one driving the horse, and he tried to persuade Uncle David otherwise. David was not to be deterred... the school had a nice barn and water for the horse and it would be good experience for the kids during the spring months. He gave Dante precise instructions about feeding and watering the horse at noontime.

Things seemed to be going well, until one night at the supper table Olivia quite innocently inquired why her dad, every morning, bring out a little bag of something, and place it in the back of the buggy, and why did Dante slow down on the way home every afternoon, and empty whatever it was out in the ditch? Dante lowered his head. David frowned. Felicity's eyes grew alarmed. "What is in the bag?" Olivia asked. Dante cringed.

"Oats," David replied. "Yes, oats for old Fan's dinner at noon, but it seems she isn't getting her dinner. What do you have to say, Dante?"

Dante kept his head down, and mumbled "Sorry."

"Sorry?" replied David. "Do you realize that old mare needs her oats, and more than that, she needs a drink of water at noon? Explain," he insisted. And, reluctantly, Dante told his story.

Noontime was when the boys played baseball, and Dante was their best pitcher, and a left-handed one at that! He didn't have time to run out, feed Fan, get water from the school cistern, and take it out. He only had forty-five minutes to play. He didn't even bother eating his own lunch! David and Felicity looked at one another. This was the first time Dante had ever caused even a small problem, and so they were perplexed. It wasn't as if David hadn't explained the importance of the old mare getting her oats and water. He had done so! Not smiling, they told Dante they would think it over and come up with a suitable penalty. They were both actually thrilled that he was interested in baseball. This was something he hadn't shared with them. David smiled as he told Felicity that as a boy, he too would not have wanted to waste any valuable time if he were part of a baseball team, and only had forty-five minutes to play. But they also knew the importance of feeding old Fan, and the wrongness of disobeying.

Dante had to realize the seriousness of what he had done. Felicity thought that maybe he could start by helping Kenshin wash and candle the eggs after school (a very tedious job), or maybe he could help Eiko weed the garden (a job she herself detested), and David laughed. He told Felicity he had the perfect position for Dante... he would take him to the field, and teach him to drive the big truck! "That's a punishment?" she asked.

"No, I don't feel this boy needs to be punished. He is feeling bad enough, and we want him to play baseball, don't we? Let's just leave it at that. He's been after me to teach him to drive, so I think it is time." In agreement with his uncle's decision, Dante acknowledged his wrongdoing. He even apologized to old Fan, although old Fan didn't seem to recognize his apology.

CHAPTER EIGHT

BACK TO PROVIDENCE!

By the spring of 1954, life had settled into a contented routine. It seemed everyone, except Felicity, was happy in their respective roles. David was busy building up his herd of Thoroughbred horses and buying cattle; Kenshin was tending to the farm, yard, and garden; and Eiko was gardening, canning, cooking, and sewing for the girls. She was always trying new recipes and inviting the Carringtons over. Dante was playing ball; and Olivia was writing and sewing on the new Pfaff electric machine they had purchased for her. The twins, Ami and Mai, were busy raising a calf with the 4H club, and both of them sang in the school choir. It was ideal, but Felicity, who couldn't resist the rich food, found it hard to keep her weight down. She didn't work as hard on the farm anymore, and wondered if the time had come for her to go back to work at the hospital in Moose Jaw, where she had taken her training prior to marrying David.

She was welcomed with open arms by Sister Mary Cornelius, who was still the Director of Nursing, and by her old mentor, Sister

Mary Raphael, who was not a nursing sister, but Mother Superior of the Sisters of Providence. Felicity was told she could pick any ward she wanted to work on, and also the shifts she wanted. Three shifts a week on the children's ward was what she asked for, and what she got! She was amazingly excited to go back to her nursing, and because it fit so well into their schedule, and with the Akiras on the farm, everything seemed so much easier! Eiko was only too pleased to keep an eye on Olivia and Dante, who in turn would help keep the twins occupied.

Felicity flourished in her new job. She had never worked on the children's ward before, but with two of her own, she found that this was certainly where God had positioned her, and needed her!

Little ones, finding it so hard to be separated from their parents, found love and comfort in Nurse Felicity. She was quick to hold and cuddle them and soothe their tiny foreheads after crying for Mom and Dad for what seemed like hours. She was particularly drawn to one little girl who had been admitted to the hospital three times in the past few months. She had been a premature baby and it seemed that her lungs were weak. She was frequently admitted with pneumonia, and kept in an oxygen tent. She would stand at the iron-railed crib in her little hospital gown and ask for Mommy: "Mommy back soon?"

Felicity would frequently hold her and tell her in a soft voice, "Mommy will be here in the morning." Sometimes she would take the little girl out and rock her in the big padded rocking chair that was kept in the towel room.

Another time a young girl was brought in who had suffered a bad fall off a horse clocked at running over eighty miles per hour. Her face, chin, and arms were cut badly, and she was traumatized by the fall. She was slated to be in her sister's wedding party in a few days. The ribs on her left side had also been damaged in the fall. Eventually, intercostal neuritis had set in. This required the young girl to take some treatments under an ultraviolet ray light, with her chest exposed. She was taken down to the X-ray machine where the procedure would take place, but when the time came for her to lower her gown to the waist, she refused. She was a shy and quiet girl, but she was adamant. Sister Mary Raphael, after unsuccessful attempts to convince or threaten the girl, took it upon herself to call the child's mother and tell her she must come to the hospital and get her daughter under control, immediately. The mother drove in from out of town, but to no avail. The young girl would not comply. As a result, the flannelette top stayed on, her face and eyes were covered up, and the strength of the light was turned up. Felicity understood this young girl was neither stubborn nor rebellious... she was just very, very shy!

Sister Mary Raphael had been at Providence Hospital for many years, and was known to be very strict. She was a devout nun, very established in her ways. She moved silently around the hospital, her black robes swishing as she walked, keeping everyone on their toes, whenever she might show up!

One day, walking by the door to this girl's room, Sister found her intently engrossed in reading a *True Confessions* magazine. Another magazine, *True Love*, lay on the bed beside her. Sister Mary Raphael was appalled. Without a word, she quickly grabbed both magazines out of the girl's hands and forbade her to read them again. Most distraught over this, Sister reached up and laid the magazines on top of a very high old wooden clothes cupboard that nearly every room in the hospital had. "Now, do not let me see you reading those again, young lady," she uttered in her very effective voice of authority. Then she left the room, her black robes swishing as she disappeared down the hallway!

The young girl lay on her bed for long time, knowing she was not allowed out of bed, and that there was no one around whom she might ask to help her. Then she gingerly got up, crawled to the end of the bed, stood up on her tiptoes, and, balanced precariously, reached her left arm over to the top corner of the cupboard. By inching a little further and extending her fingers, she managed to grab the corners of the two magazines! Just as she stepped back on the bed, there she was again: Sister Mary Raphael in person! The magazines were swiftly taken out of the room by Sister. The next day the girl's mother came to visit and her daughter told about the magazines. Upon leaving the hospital, her mother ran directly into Sister Mary Raphael, and in no uncertain terms told Sister that she herself had purchased the magazines for her daughter, and would she kindly return them to her? Sister nodded her head in agreement, but according to the daughter, they were never returned!!

CHAPTER NINE

BASEBALL AND ELVIS

OVER THE YEARS, THERE WERE TIMES WHEN BOTH FELICITY AND David had urged Dante to take up the violin. They always spoke of his father, who had been a concert violinist in Italy and in Toronto. They assured Dante that Moose Jaw wouldn't be too far to travel for lessons, but this side of forcing him, he just wasn't interested. He would sometimes take out the treasured violin that had once belonged to his father, and hold it almost reverently up to his chin and finger it... but it was always laid back into the case in favour of a baseball card or some baseball statistics! Dante lived and breathed for the game, and anyone who was willing to talk about it or show any interest at all was his best friend. Kenshin appreciated baseball, so he and Dante became fast associates hovering over the radio. Their heads were always together listening, discussing strategies, and cheering when the New York Yankees scored! David remembered that Nicholas, Dante's father, had loved baseball. It was natural, wasn't it, that his son would love the game also? David, Dante, and Kenshin regularly found themselves visiting Wilcox, Rouleau, and

Briercrest to attend the local games, and they also drove into Moose Jaw to watch the Mallards play. They even travelled into Regina to watch the Regina Red Sox!

"Maybe next year we'll see about getting you a tryout for the local travelling league in Moose Jaw. I've been told you're a pretty good lefty," David said. Dante was thrilled, and come spring that next year, David was as good as his promise. Dante made a local team in Moose Jaw, and Kenshin, with his love and savvy of the game, took it upon himself to be his own personal coach! Dante did well, and his reputation as a left-handed pitcher allowed him to advance to a secure position on the team.

In the summer of 1955, when Dante was going into grade eleven, Ken Shaw, a scout from the Brooklyn Dodgers, was sitting in the benches at a game in Regina. Dante threw a no-hitter, beating the Regina team three nothing. After the game, Shaw approached Dante and indicated his interest in signing him when he was out of school. Dante quickly called David and Kenshin over and introduced them to Shaw. It seemed Shaw was more than interested. He had talked to various coaches who had recommended Dante, and he was ready to sign him up with the Dodger Farm Team as soon as he graduated from high school the following year. Arrangements were made. Shaw would contact Dante and the Carringtons, if that was okay with Dante. Dante assured him politely that it was okay with him. Later, over milkshakes at Dairy Queen, Dante shared, even in his excitement, that he would have preferred to sign up with his favourite team, the New York Yankees.

Everyone laughed! They were all overwhelmed with the news, especially Kenshin. In a very serious voice he announced to everyone, "I have switched my loyalties. From this day forward, I will have a new favourite team: the Brooklyn Dodgers!" David agreed, laughing, that he too would be switching sides. A couple of days later, David arrived home from Regina with a brand new fourteen-inch RCA Victor television set. He said that if Dante would be making the professional team, they needed to be able to keep track of him!

Olivia was excited about the new television, but for a different reason. That year everyone had been hearing about the singing sensation "Elvis Presley", and he was scheduled to appear on *The Ed Sullivan Show* in September. All the kids at school were just counting the days till it would happen. She and Dante asked if some of the kids from school could come to the farm to watch Elvis perform on live television, and before they realized it, their plans had blossomed into a large party.

Troubled by allergies all her life, Olivia had never been a strong girl, but in these past few years, she had done remarkably well. However, just days before the Elvis event, she began to show signs of weakness. Her eyes were bothering her. Her chest was tight and she was wheezing. She tried hiding her symptoms from her mother, but they were quite obvious to everyone. At the breakfast table on Saturday morning, Felicity told her to get ready. They would be going to the emergency ward. Olivia, absolutely furious, stomped her feet at her mother. She would not do anything that would result in her missing Elvis on TV the next night! And that was that! Both David and Felicity were amazed at the resistance from this tiny quiet girl of theirs. Finally, David intervened and insisted she be taken to see the doctor. A consult with the allergist confirmed asthma as well as bronchial pneumonia. Olivia pleaded with her mother not to let the doctor admit her, especially not now! "Elvis will be on TV tomorrow night," she cried, "and I have waited months to see him sing!" Nevertheless, that afternoon she found herself hospitalized on the children's ward, with an intravenous needle in her arm, along with a warning not to get out of bed. Olivia was acquainted with a few of the nurses at the Providence Hospital, as her mother worked part time on the Children's ward.

Her anger and resentment escalated until shortly after eight p.m. the next night, when she could hear the sound of Elvis singing, "Don't be Cruel" and "Love Me Tender" coming from the TV in the hospital solarium. She wasn't allowed to get out of bed. At that moment, Olivia experienced the first stirrings of unrestrained anger, and she consciously resolved that she would never forgive her mother for this. She could have waited for two days. Olivia didn't seem aware of the acute symptoms she was experiencing. It didn't seem to matter to her that she was very sick, and her body needed healing. She fully resented the idea of someone else imposing their will on hers!

Felicity was deeply concerned about her daughter. She remembered her own father's diagnosis with depression. Could this depression be hereditary? With this question, she began analyzing her daughter in her mind. Olivia was a good girl, and rarely did anything wrong, but she seemed to carry a secret. She absolutely hated being told what to do, and she couldn't handle being teased in any way. She had been teased repeatedly at school because she wasn't sports-minded. Her allergies required her to use eye drops. Her hair always had to be short, because she was allergic to it. She loved horses, but was allergic to animal dander. Felicity wondered if her daughter's resentment was subconscious. Felicity knew that in her own way, Olivia wanted to be good, but she did not like to be told to be good. Resentment was a secret sin she carried, the kind that rarely hurts others. But if she continued this way, the bitterness could destroy her.

All of her friends would be gathering together in her living room to enjoy the party she had planned, and she wouldn't be there! This loss would be engraved in her mind, subconsciously, as her first step into jealousy, unforgiveness, and depression. This was her first step down a path that would control her life for many years.

CHAPTER TEN

GRADUATION AND GOODBYE

THE SCHOOL WAS ABLAZE WITH CHATTER ABOUT THE UPCOMING graduation plans, and the fact that their hero and friend, Dante Castrinni, was leaving for the farm team at Vero Beach Florida where he would try out for the Brooklyn Dodgers baseball team. Dresses were discussed, as well as hair, shoes, and corsages, but prominent in the minds of the graduates was the question of who Dante Castrinni would bring as his escort for his grade twelve graduation. Olivia felt herself suddenly "quite popular" at this time. She was forever being invited to chat with the older girls about Dante's plans. It made her laugh. Girls who had totally ignored the grade ten student were suddenly friendly and eager for her input, if she had any. She couldn't really help them, because she didn't know Dante's plans. She mentioned this to Felicity one evening, and together they decided they should find out Dante's plans, because three days after graduation he would be leaving for Florida, and there was a lot to get ready for! That night at the supper table, Felicity asked Dante about his plans for graduation. "We know you have ordered a white sport coat, supposedly for your graduation, but who are you inviting as your escort?"

He replied, nonchalantly, that he hadn't invited anyone, but he had a girl in mind. Olivia cautioned him that he should ask her soon, because she would have to get a dress and make an appointment to have her hair done. Olivia was curious herself as to who Dante would take. It wasn't that he didn't like girls. He did. But he liked baseball better, so he had never attached himself to any of the girls in his class. There were a couple of girls who seemed to be in attendance at every game he played, but he just wasn't interested. He made it quite obvious that girls weren't a priority on his schedule. Later that night he knocked on Olivia's bedroom door. He entered to find her lying on her bed, looking at dresses in Eaton's catalogue. "What are you looking for, Livvy?" he asked.

"Nothing, just looking."

He looked at her intently and asked, "Livvy, would you like to be my escort for grad? I always intended on asking you, but I didn't know I had to ask you so early. Would you?"

Olivia gasped, and grabbed him in a bear hug. "Yes, yes, I would. I can't believe you would ask me. Do you mean it? You won't change your mind at the last minute, will you? Are you sure you want me, Dante?" He laughed, and said he'd be back in a minute. Olivia was ecstatic! Now, she would be the envy of most of the high school girls. Dante returned with a small blue box which he handed to Olivia. She opened it to find, on a bed of white fluff, a delicate silver charm bracelet with two charms. One was a silhouette of a girl's face, with "Olivia" engraved on the back, and another was of a boy's face, with "Dante" engraved on the back.

"I was going to save this for grad night, but you can have it now. I want you to know how much I love you, Livvy. You are the sister I never had, and I will always be your champion. I will always be there for you, Livvy!"

Now Olivia was the one worrying about her hairdo and her dress. It was already the middle of June, and graduation was on June 30th.

Dante would be leaving for Florida on July 2nd, so a trip to the city must be fitted in immediately. She was up late that night looking at dresses in the Simpson, Sears, and Eaton's catalogues. She found a couple that she liked. Her mom had promised to take her to Moose Jaw the next weekend, and they would get a dress and shoes. She also decided that she wouldn't reveal to anyone who Dante would be taking to grad; it would be a surprise to everyone.

The shopping day arrived, and she chose a dress of pale blue taffeta with a wide cummerbund at the waist, short sleeves, and a full skirt with a silver thread running through it. This dress was made for her. It fit perfectly. She also bought her first pair of black suede high heel shoes. She knew she would have to practice walking in them in order to get through the grand march! She was excited about going to the grad, but even so, a dark cloud hung over the anticipation of the festivities. She held hidden anger in her heart towards her mother, and the fact that Dante would be departing shortly after graduation. And when would he come home? Would he ever come home?

In Moose Jaw, Olivia went to the new hair design salon that had just opened on Main Street. The latest style of the day was called "The Beehive", and that is what she chose. All of her dark hair was trimmed and a some hightlights added, making the short cut extremely endearing! Felicity told her she looked "spectacular", and David agreed! That night, there were several "oohs and ahhs" when she walked into the school on Dante's arm. In fact, she was hardly recognized by many of her school friends. Olivia had never been one to dress in a ladylike fashion. Blue jeans and t-shirts were her favourites! Dressed in her new blue dress and her high-heeled shoes (which she had practiced walking in) and wearing Dante's delicate bracelet on her wrist, Olivia felt as enchanted as Cinderella and Snow White all in one! The night was terrific, but she thought that saying goodbye to her cousin would be one of the hardest thing she had ever done!

July 2nd was quick to arrive! Dante was leaving for Florida! The Carringtons along with many of their friends from Drinkwater lined the platform of the CPR Train station in Moose Jaw to bid "goodbye and good luck" to the young hopeful. They didn't know how long he would be gone, or how he would do. He would be meeting many of his baseball idols, including Sandy Koufax. They would miss him dreadfully, though they were all so proud of him! Dante was surprised at his emotions that morning. He was very excited about this venture, and had spent days just imagining what the experience might be like, but he hadn't realized how hard it would be to say goodbye. He realized he had a few tears of his own as he hugged Aunt Felicity and Olivia goodbye, but when Uncle David embraced him, he cried openly.

For Kenshin, words couldn't describe his feelings as he hugged Dante. "Sayonara, Tomodachi!" he cried, hugging him tightly.

The train ride was unforgettable. First, Dante was shown to his seat and the berth that would be his for the duration of the four-day trip. Sleep was impossible as the train sped into the radiant prairie sunset. Late into the night, he reflected on the fortunate experience that he was embarking on. His gratitude went to the Lord Jesus Christ. He prayed that he would be a testimony to the witness of Christ as he ventured out on this exciting path. If Dante had been able to remember his father, he would have been surprised by how much he looked and acted like him. Uncle David often talked to Dante about his parents and when they had visited the farm many years ago. They, along with their young son, had committed their lives to Christ. One Sunday morning at the local Sunday school, Dante, at the early age of four, had invited Jesus into his heart. He reflected how God had kept his hand in his life, and he rejoiced that his desire to play baseball was on the brink of being fulfilled. He silently prayed for strength to be a witness to his heavenly Father while he was in Florida.

It was quite a dream for a young man to travel to the U.S. to play ball. He would trust the Lord for wisdom and strength in the coming days. Going to the dining car the next morning, he saw for the first time Negro stewards, with dazzling white jackets and white towels folded over their arms, waiting on tables and taking orders for meals. The tables were covered in the whitest tablecloths he had ever seen with small bouquets of fresh flowers on each table! Tall pitchers of ice water and orange juice had been placed on each table as well. After ordering breakfast, he was brought two fried eggs, over easy; three long slices of crisp bacon that nearly covered the plate; and a sliced orange garnishing one side of the plate, along with small sprig of what he later found out to be parsley, as a decorative gesture. Toast and hot steaming coffee rounded out the attractive meal. This was very impressive for a young man of seventeen.

During his long trip to Florida, Dante had plenty of time to visit with other passengers and dream of his future with his new "favourite team", as he remembered Kenshin saying! He wondered about meeting

Sanford "Sandy" Koufax , a new left-handed pitcher for the Dodgers!

CHAPTER ELEVEN

THE ITALIANS VISIT

ONE AFTERNOON, JUST TWO WEEKS AFTER DANTE HAD LEFT FOR Vero Beach, Florida, Felicity happened to glance out the east window and notice a bright yellow taxi cab drive into the yard. She had no idea who would be coming to the farm in a taxi. She watched, astounded, as Steophano Castrinni and his two sisters stepped out of the car! She silently wished David were home today.

Felicity invited them in. She noticed the taxi remained waiting, in the yard. After offering refreshments of cold lemonade, she boldly asked the reason for their visit. "We are here to see the boy," replied Steophano.

Instantly she bristled, and said, "His name is Dante, not the boy, as you have always referred to him. He isn't here. He is in Florida playing baseball." The expressions on their faces said they were surprised and definitely not pleased. Steophano seemed at a loss for words, and the two sisters began to speak in rapid and almost perfect English.

"Why is he out of the country? How is his school going? What grade is he in? Is he playing the violin?"

Inundated by the questions, Felicity shook her head in bewilderment. She remembered the long blue envelopes that arrived monthly, with never a question about Dante's wellbeing, or any information in regards to his Italian relatives. "Why now?" she wondered.

Without waiting for an answer, Steophano spoke. Their father, Michael Castrinni, was dying, and wanted to see his grandson before he died. Grandmother Gaetane was getting old, and wanted to end the estrangement of her only grandson. Steophano explained to Felicity that it had been the family's choice, over the years, not to get in touch with the boy, because they knew if they got to know him personally, they would get attached, and it would be too heartbreaking for them if they had to let him return to Canada. Felicity did not believe this! "Michaelo and Gaetane are old now," continued Steophano, "and Nicholas, the boy's father, had been their youngest son, born in the later years of their life." When Nicholas had moved to Canada with Merrin all those years ago, the family were all heartbroken, especially the parents. It had been their plan to leave everything to young Nicholas when he reached the age of twenty-five, but by that time, he had already left with Merrin for Canada and another life! Both Elena and Bianca were married to very influential businessmen, and they were independently wealthy in their own rights. Mimi, the youngest daughter, had graduated from the University of Rome as a veterinarian, and had moved to Peru to conduct animal research. Steophano had purchased a business in Venezuela and had planned on taking up residence there, but when Nicholas left so suddenly, he was required to stay in Italy and work in the family's winery business. It seemed that no one in the immediate family had an interest in the Castrinni heritage, nor in caring for the grandparents at this time in their lives. The parents had intended on this being Nicholas' lot in life, although it was never discussed with him. It was just assumed, and expected, on their parts. "After all," continued Steophano, "he was the youngest. He would move back home to Florence. All of their property, villas, the winery, everything would be his! He would be a welcome addition to the local symphony orchestra, and no doubt find a wife and settle down! In any case, the family had spent a considerable amount of money in supporting his musical career over the years. Special lessons! Very expensive! They felt outraged and betrayed at the turn of events."

Bianca Pacorro spoke almost inaudibly, in a voice of a confessor, "Yes, we did not treat Merrin Towers well. We saw her as a threat to our plans, and for that we are very sorry!! Could the Carringtons forgive us?" she pleaded. "We desperately want Dante to get to know his grandparents before they both die. Would David and Felicity help us get Dante to Italy to become acquainted with his grandparents?"

Felicity didn't trust them, considering how they had treated her sister. She didn't like the fact that over the years they had never responded to Dante as their nephew, other than the monthly allowances they sent. Never a letter, or personal inquiry of his welfare.

She had always speculated at their motives, and she wondered at the fact that the sisters now spoke fluent English. Had it all been an act those many years ago at the funeral, or had they recently learned English? For her own satisfaction, she needed to know, and so she bluntly asked, "When you came to Toronto for the funeral, what were your plans? You never spoke directly to David or myself, and would only converse with Michael Gallo, Nicholas' lawyer. We understood then that you women only spoke Italian. Am I correct in my recollections? All three of you were adamant on taking Dante away, and it is only because Michael Gallo spoke out on our behalf that you relented. Why would you only refer to him as 'the boy', Mr. Castrinni? You are still referring to him as 'the boy'. You are still not calling him by his name, which is Dante. I demand answers to these questions before we go any farther in this conversation."

Bianca replied, in excellent English, "Mrs. Carrington, it is true; we acted superior and condescending to you and your husband when we came to Toronto, and over the intervening years. We were advised by our parents not to engage in a conversation with either of you, but to let our brother be responsible for all conversations! Yes, we children all speak English; some of us better than others! We admit to you that we were wrong in our attitudes in Toronto. We did not listen to you or your husband. We were set in our ways, and we did more harm than good. The way of the Castrinni family is not a good way, but a selfish way, never listening to the hearts and desires of others. I see how receiving the money every month, without inquiring about how our nephew Dante" (Felicity noticed the inflection on the name Dante) "was doing. We have been dreadfully wrong. We are proud people, but today we are asking for your forgiveness." Felicity couldn't respond immediately, and Bianca said again in a voice quivering with emotion, "We are asking your forgiveness, and desperately wanting you to hear our hearts."

Where was David when you needed him? Felicity remembered that day years ago, when she was alone in Merrin's home in Toronto and the Castrinnis came to the door. As a Christian, she knew that forgiveness was not an option, nor was it based on a feeling. It was a commandment, and God's will to forgive. She would! She had no choice! As she was mulling this over in her mind, Steophano asked again, "Where is the boy?" Again, not using Dante's name.

"I told you," said Felicity, "he is in Florida, in the United States, trying out at a baseball camp. He is a pitcher! A left-handed pitcher!" She smiled proudly. The three Castrinnis exchanged puzzled looks. A baseball camp? What was he doing at a baseball camp? Felicity tried explaining, but they weren't listening! They resumed speaking Italian, and she could tell they were more than upset. All three were resolute in their disapproval of letting him leave the country to pursue a career in baseball. They asked where the money came from to finance such a venture, as they sincerely hoped it didn't come from the funds they had forwarded over the years! At this point, Felicity had a hard time keeping her temper intact. "Lord, I am ready to explode at the nerve of these people."

Years of anger and torment surged through her mind, and yet a still, small overpowering voice urged her to hold her emotions in check. In a controlled voice, she explained that David had paid for Dante to travel to the U.S. She went on to assure them that a career in professional baseball could prove to be very lucrative. If he was the "pitching star" as they thought him to be, his starting salary could be very high! David would even be reimbursed by the Dodger Baseball Association for the cost of the trip. She went on to reassure them that Dante in his own right was "quite well-off", having never spent a cent of the money they had sent over. In addition, the money from the estate of his parents had been wisely invested, and was growing interest, resulting in a profitable nest egg that was available to him and could be easily accessed should a need arise! The family were aghast! A look of what she thought was absolute betrayal was on their faces. Felicity was weary of these people who thought only of themselves.

Elena, the elder sister who had not yet spoken a word, put up her hand in what could be interpreted as "a sign of peace" and tried to persuade Felicity to please listen to what they called "our side of the story". She said, "Please, please Felicity... I remember that you spoke of being a born-again Christian. I have studied the Holy Bible, and yes, I have found it in the blessed book of the Apostle John. You say you are born again, and that you have received salvation through a personal relationship with Jesus Christ. I implore you, dear Felicity, please hear us as we humbly ask forgiveness for the treatment of your sister Merrin many years ago, and for being cold and isolated when we came for the funeral. We were so bereft in our grief and resolute in our desire that our plans go according to the wishes of our parents, the way we had all decided, without consulting our dear Nicholas. We all expected Nicholas to fall into our plans, and it was not to be! I beg of you, Felicity, our parents are old and Father is dying; his heart is weak, and he wants to see Dante. Please help us. Do what you can to make this happen for them!"

Felicity heard the heart of Elena Paccorro in just that moment. "I'm sorry," she said, "we don't really know when he will be coming home. He is in the training camp right now, and if he makes the team, he will be getting a U.S. work visa, or green card, and be assigned to a team. You will have to reach him by phone, or go to Florida." The Castrinnis looked defeated in their silence. Felicity waited for them to huddle together like last time, but they didn't. All three looked so dissatisfied and completely out of their element. She wondered where they were staying, and how long they planned on being in Canada.

Again, Felicity's mind flashed back to her sister Merrin describing the hostility and coolness she had received from the Castrinni family on her first visit to Italy, many years ago. "Where do we go from here?" she asked herself. Her mind was filled with questions.

Dante was aware of his family in Italy, as both David and Felicity had told him about them coming to the funeral, and wanting to take him back to Italy. He knew how much they had loved their youngest brother, Nicholas, Dante's father, as well as his mother Merrin. David and Felicity had never once revealed a negative sentiment in regards to their feelings towards the Castrinni family in Italy. As a young boy, Dante would always smile and say he was glad Uncle David and Aunt Felicity had taken him home, because he loved the farm. As he grew older it seemed the events of the day, and his love of baseball, had overcome any feelings of the Italian family he had never met.

Thankfully, David arrived and graciously welcomed the Castrinnis to his home. Before anyone had a chance to say anything, Felicity shared the reason for their impromptu visit. Now it was David's turn to feel perplexed, and yet there had always been the realization that one day, this would happen. "Dante isn't here, as you already know," said David, "but it would be good for you to meet him and talk to him in person. Unfortunately, we don't know when he will be home again, or where he really is right now! We're all hoping he will make the Dodgers team, in which case he will be headquartered in Brooklyn, but we won't know for another two or three more weeks." Silence... disappointment... confusion as to what to do now covered their faces. Steophano especially looked puzzled. It was Felicity who broke the silence.

"You asked me to forgive you for the altercations we have shared, in regards to my sister, and to Dante, over the years. I do forgive you. I know that Dante is a part of your lives; he is your nephew as well, and he is a wonderful young man. You should get to know him! Please, sit down and let's talk this over and see what solution we can come up with. Please, sit down, relax, and I will get us some tea." They did sit down, although in a rigid and mechanical way. Noticing the taxi was waiting in the yard, Felicity invited them to stay for a few days. But again, in no uncertain terms, they told her they would be leaving soon. Felicity shook her head, and decided she had said and done enough. She left the room, leaving David to handle this.

Steophano opened up to David that they weren't able to go to Florida at this time, and would David place a call to Dante and tell him of the family's circumstances, and see what the boy might do? David was not a contentious man. He was not one to hold a grudge, but this time he again felt he could not submit to the Castrinnis' request. He asked, "Why didn't you inform us you were coming over, and ask if Dante would be home?" But these questions seemed to fall on deaf ears.

Bianca stood, and looked directly at David. "Will you call him for us?" she implored.

"No," David replied. "I'm sorry. I will not call him. He has a lot on his mind these days. You have disregarded him for over seventeen years, and these next two weeks are very crucial to his career. I am sorry for your circumstances, and that your father is ill, but you have had years to build a relationship with Dante. I will certainly give you his contact number; I can't withhold that from you. But I know that the tryouts are hard, and your call would no doubt upset him."

Bianca asked in a whisper, "Is he a good boy?"

"Yes," David replied sincerely, "he is a very good boy."

Looking directly at his sisters, Steophano Castrinni motioned for them to leave, and they silently walked out of the house and got into the waiting taxi without a word of goodbye or explanation. David followed, asking if they wanted Dante's telephone number in Florida. Steophano shook his head, again looking overwhelmed, and ever so slowly got into the taxi and closed the door. David and Felicity watched the taxi drive down the grid road until it went over the hill. They looked at each other, and then silently, as if God had spoken, they bowed their heads in prayer. As a family the Castrinnis were very dysfunctional, in many ways. They were hurting desperately, and in need of Christ's healing touch upon their lives. The visit left the Carringtons at a loss. The Castrinnis were Dante's family. Michaelo Castrinni was his paternal grandfather, and he was dying, so Steophano had said. Should they call Dante and inform him? David said he would pray about the decision, and they went about their day.

That evening David put in a call to the Dodger camp. Dante wasn't around at the time but word was left for him to call home, whenever he had a moment, but it was not an emergency. It wasn't until the next afternoon he called. As David relayed the story of the family's visit, Dante was surprised that they had come to the farm, without any prior notice! He was aware of his inheritance, as just before he left for Florida, both David and Felicity had sat him down and shared all the details, but he had never received any communication from the family in Italy. He told David that he was definitely being signed by the Dodgers, and this would be under official contract within the next day or so! He was jubilant! He definitely could not go to Italy now. He was having the time of his life. Plans to go to Italy, under any circumstances, would be placed on hold until the season was over.

CHAPTER TWELVE

THE BANK BOOKS!

EVERYONE MISSED DANTE, BUT NO ONE MORE THAN OLIVIA. THE first cousins been close throughout their young lives, like brother and sister. One afternoon, as she went by his room, she casually opened the door. She could just imagine him sitting at his desk, doing homework, reading, or whatever. She lay down on his bed and looked around. Noticing the posters on the wall of Mickey Mantle and Don Larsen, of the New York Yankees, she thought to herself, "Dante, you had better get some posters of the Dodgers in here soon!" and she laughed at the thought. She picked up his school jacket and smelled the familiar scent of his favourite aftershave, Old Spice. Oh, how she wished he were home. She casually wandered around his room, picking up this and that, and found herself sitting at his old desk. She pushed up the roll top and was surprised at the neatness of the contents. Without thinking she opened one of the pull-out drawers, and her eyes fell on a manila envelope, containing two bank books, lying side by side. She didn't hesitate to pick them up and open them.

The wine-coloured one from the Commerce Bank showed a balance of twenty-eight thousand, five hundred and forty-six dollars, and ninety-seven cents. Olivia was stunned! She couldn't believe her eyes. Then, she opened the blue-coloured Royal Bank book, and she felt shivers run up her back. This could not be true. It showed a balance of one hundred and thirteen thousand, four hundred and thirty-seven dollars, and sixty-two cents. There was also a letter addressed to Dante, in care of her parents, showing the accumulated interest and principal on an initial investment opened in December of 1942 for well over eighty thousand dollars. Quickly she added up the figures in her head, and realized this was over two hundred thousand dollars. Where on earth had Dante gotten that kind of money? Lying beside the bank books was a fairly large brown envelope addressed to Mr. Dante Nicholas Castrinni, in care of Mr. and Mrs. David Carrington. Again, she didn't hesitate to open the envelope. Inside she found a statement of what looked like a deed to a place in Florence, Italy called the Villa Val di Pesa. She was stunned at this discovery, and for the second time in her young life, she reacted with near rage! She felt strong emotions of overpowering covetousness, and resentment, and yet, at the same time, she was shaken by her negative reaction. She immediately thought of her Royal Bank account which had a balance of thirty-seven dollars and sixty cents, at the present time. Where did this money come from, and why had Dante never told her about it? Why had her parents never told her about it? Why the secrecy? She placed the statement back into the envelope, along with the two bank books where she had found them, and left the room. She couldn't remember any "secrets" in her family, and yet she had never been aware of Dante's fortune. She couldn't shake the feelings of betrayal, and also the guilt of knowing her feelings and reactions were wrong. After all, she had no business snooping in his room, and going through the drawers of his desk. Because of this, she knew she wouldn't be asking her parents to explain, and felt guilty about that also!

Several times in the next few days, Olivia found herself wanting to ask her mother about Dante's money, but she never did. Every time she thought about it, feelings of pride and anger, as well as guilt, would flare up, causing her to feel distressed. She had never in her life felt any type of jealousy towards Dante. She idolized him! He was her champion! But still, the anger! Or was it pride? She was well aware that both she and Dante had always been treated as equals, although Olivia's wasn't required to do farm chores, there were chores in the house, that were designated as her's. For this, they were given an allowance. She remembered time and time again her dad calling them in to give them their allotted allowance, and how she and Dante could hardly wait to go to town to spend it. They were both generous, and would invite whoever was around to share in their rewards. Tootsie Rolls, Jersey Milk bars, and Burnt Almond chocolate bars were five cents, as were Popsicles and Revels. Black Jawbreakers were one cent. A glass bottle of Coca-Cola was five cents to drink in the store and seven cents if you took the bottle. Sometimes she would come home with a small brown bag filled with penny candy, which she would always share with Ami and Mai.

Dante would sometimes save his allowance, with a certain goal in mind. He bought a little transistor radio, a guitar, a pair of skates, and not so long ago a white sports jacket to wear to his graduation. All this time, he had a fortune in the bank. Olivia struggled with her feelings, knowing them to be wrong. Dante's secret fortune annoyed her, and she didn't know why. And at the same time, the anger seemed to be directed once again to her mother.

One afternoon, in frustration, she told her best friend Marlene about this "mystery money", as she referred to it. Marlene told Olivia that she remembered a couple of years ago when her mother had commented on the "blue envelopes" that came from Italy every month, and the attractive stamps! Could this be where Dante got the money? Olivia thought this was a plausible explanation, because along with the two bank books there was a letter about a villa in

Italy. Maybe the money was from his Italian relatives! And if it was, why hadn't he shared this secret with her?

She began to realize that it was the fact that Dante hadn't shared this with her that was also causing the bitterness and jealousy in her heart. They had always shared everything. They were confidants, but apparently not in regards to "the money".

Olivia's anger was apparent, and she made no excuse for it. When Marlene questioned her about her attitude, she realized that even though Olivia could present a fairly calm exterior, she possessed a very silent temper. Her anger simmered! It was obvious to Marlene, who had known her for many years and who had spent many hours at the farm, that Olivia did not like to be criticized or corrected in any way. Marlene was extremely concerned about her friend and this caused her great turmoil. She had talked to her mom about the changes that had been occurring in Olivia, and together they had both recognized a serious problem. At this time, Marlene told Olivia in a very composed sixteen-year-old voice that she had recognized a change in Olivia that wasn't good. "Why do you resist your parents? This isn't how Jesus would want you to act, Olivia, and you know that. Your parents are good to you." Marlene went on to say that she hurt every time Olivia overlooked them, and she had realized that Olivia seemed to harbour a deep animosity, especially toward her mother!

Olivia listened cautiously to Marlene, seemingly hearing her, but with a look of bewilderment on her face. She hugged Marlene, telling her that she would consider this and pray about it, but she let Marlene know, by smiling and rolling her eyes, that she didn't take this advice seriously.

Again, Olivia made a decision to keep this information to herself, and not confide in her parents. It took no time at all for this decision to work its way in the form of offence deep down into her heart. She recognized it immediately, but disregarded the prompting of the Holy Spirit, and without realizing it, was caught deeply in the trap of bitterness! She began to withdraw and seek the seclusion of her room.

When asked by her parents what was wrong, she answered that she thought her allergies were coming back and she was tired. She lost her appetite, and stopped eating. This was in September, just one year after the severe asthma attack that had put her in the hospital. She was just beginning her eleventh grade in school. Everyone admitted that the change in Olivia was subtle at first, but clearly noticeable to everyone around her, even Kenshin and Eiko. But it was the twins, Ami and Mai, who brought it out in the open when they innocently asked Felicity why Olivia didn't like them anymore. They said she didn't even talk to them at recess or lunch, and that she spent most of that time just sitting alone on the school steps.

David and Felicity were puzzled and heartsick about their daughter. They often questioned her about what was bothering her, and her reply was always the same, "I'm just not feeling up to par! Nothing to worry about!" But one day after school Olivia stopped in to see Marlene at the post office, and she had a fainting spell. Wilma Price promptly phoned Felicity who in turn made an appointment for Olivia to see the doctor at the hospital later that evening. This would be the second time Olivia openly defied her parents. She refused to go to Moose Jaw to see a doctor. Felicity was just ready to relinquish the idea and take her in the morning, but when Olivia stood up, she became faint again. The argument was over; they were going to the ER! After a brief examination, the doctor on duty suggested admitting her for a number of tests. She was extremely dehydrated, and according to the scales, there was a weight loss of close to seven pounds since her last visit.

Felicity had shared with the doctor that she and her husband were concerned, as they felt their daughter was in a depression. She explained about Dante leaving, and attributed some of Olivia's condition to that. The doctor smiled at Felicity condescendingly and said, "She is a teenager. These are simply growing pains. Don't worry about her."

Throughout the examination, Olivia remained silent and brooding. She inwardly vowed that she would not forgive her mother or

Dante for keeping her "out of the loop" in regards to Dante's fortune in the bank. She would not forgive them, and they would be sorry!

She was only sixteen years old, and already she was moving further down the subtle path of her soul's enemy. By blatantly choosing not to forgive, she had reopened the door to a bitterness that would cause irreparable changes in the plan that God had for her. Routine blood tests showed Olivia's immune system to be very weak. In addition, she had an upper respiratory infection, her electrolytes were unbalanced, her blood count was low, and there was possibly the beginning of an ulcer. Over the next few days, she was given fluids and began to improve. After a week, she was allowed to come home. She looked rather pale, and David wondered if a holiday might do her good. After talking with his mother, it was decided that Olivia could stay with her grandparents for the rest of the summer. She was delighted to go. Thrilled, she packed up almost everything she owned and her parents drove her across the border to Grandpa and Grandma Carrington's home in Montana.

She had visited them over the years, but had never stayed with them without her parents. Grandma Carrington was positively overjoyed to acquaint her granddaughter to her many friends. She went out of her way to make Olivia feel welcome and at home. With no chores to do, she was allowed to sleep late every morning. Grandma bought her new clothes. She even promised to take her out to her friend's farm and let her practice driving the new 1957 Buick that Grandpa had just bought for his wife.

Olivia had smiled as her parents left, knowing that her mother wasn't at all pleased in letting her daughter stay in Montana for the summer. Felicity wasn't as worried about Olivia's health as much as she was concerned over her sullenness and bad attitude. She had tried talking to Olivia on many different occasions, but it all seemed to fall on deaf ears. They just didn't seem to connect! But maybe David was right. He usually was! An extended holiday might be just what she needed!

CHAPTER THIRTEEN

TROUBLE IN MISSOULA

THIS TIME DAVID WAS WRONG! OLIVIA HAD OPENED THE DOOR TO trouble. Her heart was in rebellion, although she would not have been aware of it at this time. She loved being spoiled by her grandmother, and without realizing it, she took advantage of her generosity. She would drop casual hints, and Grandma, wanting to please her, would pick up on them. Once she shared with her grandma that her cousin Dante, whom she really did love, had a secret bank account, and he could do anything he wanted with the money, and how she didn't think that was fair. She had to work for her allowance. Again, this wasn't true. Olivia, because of her allergies, had been released from doing any outside work! Grandma didn't think that was fair, either, and told Olivia she would do something about that, but for now, she gave her one hundred dollars for spending money. "That was easy!" thought Olivia.

One afternoon, Olivia told her grandma she wanted to go to the mall, just to look around. She was dropped off at the mall and told she would be picked up at five p.m. She strolled around the mall for a while, and then spied some girls her age at the Orange Julius stand. She went over and before long was chatting with the three girls, whose names were Sherry, Diane, and Melissa. Thinking about it later, Olivia was surprised at her outgoing nature. Normally she was not at all sociable, but for some reason, something inside of her had changed this summer! The girls invited Olivia to go with them to the show that night, and she said she probably could. They exchanged phone numbers, promising to be in touch later, and then all of a sudden Grandma was outside waiting for her. Once inside the car, Olivia told Grandma that she had met some girls from the Baptist Church, and they had invited her to their youth group, and could she go? Grandma answered affirmatively, and later that evening, drove Olivia to meet the girls at the mall, from which point they would walk to the church together. "That got by Grandma real easy," she reflected.

    She was very much aware that she was lying to her grandmother, but it wasn't hurting anyone, was it? And for the first time, Olivia felt important!! For the next two weeks, Olivia and her new friends made arrangements and did whatever they liked. One night they went to Melissa's house when her parents weren't home. Another time Olivia called Grandma and asked if she could stay over at Sherry's overnight, but Grandma said no. This made Olivia angry at her, but she didn't let Grandma know she was angry. She seemed to be good at this! One Saturday morning, Diane hinted how great it would be if they could go to into Butte and shop. It wasn't that far away, but there was no one to take them! Olivia, without even hesitating, told them she could get her grandma's car, and she could drive. "Are you sure?" they asked her. "Do you have a licence?"

    She again didn't hesitate, but answered, "Absolutely." She told them that Gram had already let her drive her new Buick! Yes, Gram had let her drive, and Olivia had done quite well, but that was only on the dirt road on Mrs. Bailey's farm. She explained to the girls that Saturday afternoon would be the perfect time to go. Gram always went to her book reading club on Saturday afternoons, and Grandpa usually went golfing or to the ball game, if he wasn't on-call at the hospital. She had heard Gram make arrangements for her friend to pick her up this Saturday, so Olivia knew the Buick would be in the yard. "No problem," she told the girls. "Just be ready at the corner of Gram's street." She figured that they could leave at 12:30 and be home before Gram got home at 5:30.

After the arrangements had been made, and she went home, butterflies began to churn in her stomach! She had second thoughts. She wondered what Sherry, Diane, and Melissa would think if she called them back with a change of plans. But she didn't want to. For the first time in her life, she was the outgoing one, the one who had the ideas, and she liked the attention it brought her. Besides, it was only for an afternoon, and Grandma had said she was a very good driver. "I'll be able to get my driver's licence as soon as I get back home in the fall. What's to be afraid of?" Grandma was a bit concerned when Olivia said she would be spending the afternoon home alone with a good book. Olivia did feel guilty when Gram kissed her goodbye, with a promise of bringing her home a surprise.

"You're such a treasure, Olivia, and I'm so glad we've been able to get to know each other better. We so love you, dear girl!" Somehow that didn't make Olivia feel very good at all! But, plans were plans, and a promise was a promise!

As arranged, the girls were at the corner at 12:30. Sherry hopped in the front seat, and Melissa and Diane hopped in the back, and they were off. Olivia had never driven in the city, but she had driven a lot with her Gram, who was a slow and careful driver. Olivia considered she knew as much about driving as Gram did. After all, she'd been driving with her parents for years. She'd watched them carefully, hadn't she? What's to know? Finally, they were out on the highway and cruising along at about forty-five MPH, doing quite well, she told herself. Actually, she was enjoying it, and she felt so extremely important! The girls began telling stories and laughing noisily, as girls do at that age. It bothered Olivia, as she realized she had to pay close attention to the road. She asked them more than once to not be so loud, as she found she really had to concentrate while driving, and it was hard, with all the laughter going on. Plus, the girls were funny and she would have liked to join in! They began to laugh louder!

After a couple of miles, when they still weren't settling down, she unthinkingly reached over the back seat to grab Melissa, to tell her to stop. Taking her eyes off the road for just a split second, she felt the car veering to the right, and there was no way she could stop it. Into the ditch it went, hitting the passenger side with a loud whack, and then before she could take a breath, the car turned completely over and settled on its roof. It all happened in seconds, and in what seemed to be "slow motion". Melissa was flung partly into the front seat, and Sherry seemed to be laying on the dash with blood running all over her face and arms. Olivia had been pushed up onto the steering wheel, and she could feel sharp pain under her rib cage. There was no sound from Diane in the back seat. Finally, she heard Melissa crying, and suddenly Sherry tried to move. It seemed like forever until they heard Diane moaning in the back seat. Olivia was having trouble breathing, and realized she was having an asthma attack. Looking at her watch, Olivia thought maybe they had been in the ditch for maybe fifteen minutes. Out of the blue, red flashing lights drove up behind them and two highway patrol officers were crouched down, looking in the windows. By this time, Olivia was having serious trouble breathing. She realized the officers were getting the girls out of the car and up onto the highway. When they came to get her, she had nearly lost consciousness, and could feel sharp pain in her back. That was the last thing she remembered.

Later she awoke, thinking she could hear her grandpa's voice. She realized there were curtains around her bed. She also realized there was an oxygen mask on her face and she was in a hospital, and that voice she heard was that of her grandpa, Dr. Stewart Carrington. He was not playing golf, or watching a ball game. He wasn't on call, but had stopped in to see a patient of his. He was leaving through the emergency entrance when the call came in that four teenagers were being transported in from a highway accident, so he had decided to stay and offer his help if needed. He was totally unprepared and astonished to see his own granddaughter brought in from the ambulance, and her state of unconsciousness caused him total bewilderment!

When she regained consciousness, everything came flooding back to her! She had lied to Grandma about staying home alone to read, and she had lied to the girls that she had a licence. She remembered taking Grandma's new car without permission, driving on the highway, the girls laughing, hitting the ditch, the car turning over. Where were Sherry, Melissa, and Diane? Were they alright? Were they in the hospital? There was absolutely no way to get out of this state of affairs! She knew she was in serious trouble! What would Gram think? What would her parents think? What would the highway patrol think, and what would they do? She knew it wouldn't be a laughing matter, and she wondered how disappointed her dad would be. As for her mother, she knew it would be alarming for her, but her feelings towards her mother had not been first-rate lately, so she quickly pushed that thought out of her mind!

All of a sudden, her grandfather appeared from the other side of the curtain. "What ever happened, Olivia? Why were you with those girls? We don't even know them," he exclaimed. At this point, Dr. Carrington didn't know that it was his wife's new Buick that was involved in the accident. Olivia looked at her grandpa, at his snowy white hair and his handsome face. She had always loved him, although as a young child, she had been wary of his stern manner! Now, he looked at her with compassion, which in turn caused shame and embarrassment to wrap themselves around her. She knew how this would hurt her grandparents deeply, and that the outcome wouldn't be easy to explain. A nurse came in and told Dr. Carrington that X-rays showed the youngest girl, Diane Fielding, had a broken wrist that would have to be casted. She would need to remain a couple of days in the hospital for observation. The other two girls, Sherry Grey and Melissa Lewis, had minor cuts and bruises and their parents were on the way to get them. Olivia was suffering from an asthma attack and her rib cage had been badly bruised, causing considerable pain. She too would have to remain at the hospital for a couple of days.

A patrol officer popped his head around the curtain and asked to speak to Dr. Carrington. Her grandpa left. He couldn't have gotten too far before she heard him exclaim loudly, "Impossible. It couldn't be." Olivia assumed that Grandpa now knew that the car involved in the accident was Grandma's new Buick! She waited for his return, embarrassed and sorry for what she had done. She certainly could not place the blame for her actions on anyone but herself. She was definitely the instigator of this situation. Finally, Grandpa came back and looked at her enquiringly. He asked, "Tell me, Olivia, whatever made you take Grandma's car and drive it on the highway, with girls we don't even know? Why would you do that?"

Again, for whatever reason, Olivia felt the unspoken accusations against her, and the expectation to give an account for her actions. She didn't like it. In this moment she felt the same old irritation and anger rise towards her grandpa. Just moments ago, she had been mentally rehearsing the apology she would make to Grandma and Grandpa, and to her friends. She had thought about Diane's parents, and her own parents. But now, her anger instantly outweighed her remorse and regret. She did not like to be accused, and she did not like to take responsibility. And so, she stiffened her chin defiantly and irately answered her grandpa by stating, "It wasn't my fault." She lowered her eyes and stared into her folded hands, finally turning her head to the side so Grandpa would not see the tears. They were tears of regret, but she would not acknowledge her responsibility or her accountability in the situation.

"I have called your parents, and they will be here sometime tomorrow," Grandpa told her. "You get some rest and I will be back later."

Olivia reached out for his hand, and asked, "Grandpa, how are the girls? Were they hurt?" He explained their condition, and again, with an uneasy look on his face, left the curtained area.

A nurse came in and helped Olivia sit up. The nurse wrapped her rib cage with support bandages, and gave her something for the pain. Olivia was then moved to another room, where she would remain until tomorrow. She continued to wonder about the girls, especially Diane. She remembered her moaning in the back seat, and the sound of Melissa crying. She waited for the pain medication to kick in, and slowly felt herself drifting off to sleep. Her last recollection was that of Felicity's face, the day they had said goodbye. Her mother's last words had been, "Please don't cause any concern for your grandparents, Olivia!"

It was astonishing to Olivia how many lives were affected as a result of her foolish, irresponsible actions. Again, for a moment, she recognized the tug on her heart to acknowledge her mistake, but she resolutely and consciously decided to ignore her conscience. After all, it was the girls' idea to go. She had been coerced into taking them. No one had forced those girls to ride in the car. It was their decision to go with her. It simply wasn't her fault.

David and Felicity arrived in Missoula next afternoon. Before going to the hospital, David made arrangements with the Juvenile Court for his father to appear for Olivia, and pay the fine, whatever it might be, so they could take Olivia home with them immediately. They both looked extremely upset when they entered Olivia's room. She had been sitting up in a chair, and quickly averted her face from them. For a few moments no one spoke. Finally, David asked, "Why, Livvy? Why would you take your grandma's new car on the highway, and put lives in danger? Why?" There was no answer from Olivia. He explained that they would be taking her home immediately, and that he had made arrangements for the fine to be paid, etc.

She looked her father angrily in the eye and asked, in a childish voice, "You have made all these arrangements without even consulting me?"

"Of course," he said, "someone has to look after your foolishness."

"You mean you did all that before coming to see me?" she asked.

"Yes," he replied. "Grandpa said you were not badly hurt, and I'm in a hurry to get home. We are in the middle of calving. We are leaving for home right away." She moaned that she couldn't sit in the car, and that she didn't want to go home.

Felicity said curtly, "You have to come home, Olivia. Your grandparents are very upset with you, and I don't think you would be very welcome." Olivia's anger subsided for a few minutes as she thought things over. She really had messed up this time, and had deeply disappointed her family in the process.

CHAPTER FOURTEEN

GRADUATION AND CONCERNS

THE CARRINGTONS CAME HOME FROM MISSOULA WITH SCORES OF unanswered questions, and a great deal unsaid. Olivia wore a sulky and defiant look on her face most of the time. Trying to find out the root of the problem wasn't possible when conversations were always one-sided. David had paid the seventy-dollar fine at the Juvenile Court in Missoula. As for Grandma's car, and the fact that Olivia took it without permission, the police could have charged Olivia, but with Grandpa's intervention that didn't happen. They would be responsible for the damage of close to one thousand dollars. David wrote out a cheque to cover the repairs of the Buick, and sent it to his mother.

Olivia was restricted from driving Felicity's car, and she didn't even ask about getting her driver's license. In response to the question of how she would get to school, David minced no words as he explained that his plans had been to buy her a second-hand older car that she would use to drive herself and the twins to school, but because of her irresponsible behaviour, that was now out of the question! She sarcastically suggested riding her bike, and David told her, in no uncertain terms, that sounded like an excellent idea!

Her twelfth year of school began in the fall of 1959. Felicity wondered if Olivia had told any of her friends of her summer shenanigans in Missoula. But, knowing her daughter well, Felicity felt Olivia no doubt told no one. She didn't like to be seen in a negative light. It was Eiko who solved the question of getting the girls to school. She and Kenshin had a small car, and she had taken it upon herself to learn to drive around the farm a couple of years prior. She went to Moose Jaw, took her driving test, got her license, and was proud to help out in this way! Olivia adored Eiko Akira, and she eventually began confiding in her. It didn't take Eiko long to realize that whatever it was, even though her behaviour was shocking, the young girl was desperately hurting. She simply could not understand why Olivia had shut out her mother, and now it seemed her father!

After a while, Olivia began to settle down to her old self, and Felicity breathed a sigh of relief. Olivia never brought up the situation in Missoula, but she often mulled over the details of her actions in her mind. No matter how she responded on the outside, she was still angry. She was angry at being caught! She would always remember facing her grandparents the day she and her folks were returning home. Grandpa had appeared indignant, and didn't even really look at her. Grandma had looked so hurt and disappointed, but she had held Olivia in her arms and cried. Olivia told them both she was sorry for taking the car, and lying to the girls, but she couldn't give a tangible answer to Grandpa as to why she had done what she did. It seemed to her that Grandma was the most understanding of them all. She hugged Olivia goodbye, telling her that "Young people do outlandish things at times, and it could have been worse; no one was killed… Let's count our blessings." She then folded something into Olivia's hand. It wasn't until later, on the drive home, that Olivia opened the folded paper to see three one hundred American dollar bills folded up carefully. No note, just the money. For some reason, Olivia felt more guilt over this than the car accident. She had manipulated Grandma into thinking she had not been treated fairly when she had tried to explain her feelings of betrayal surrounding Dante's bank books. Looking back at her manipulative behaviour, she felt guilt-ridden.

Christmas came with blizzards, snow, and cold. Dante made it home for a few days, and found it hard adjusting to the cold weather. He mentioned more than once that his arm had been giving him problems when he threw hard, but right now, he was still their number two lefty! He found himself drawn to and very fascinated with the Thoroughbred horses David had been amassing. They were beauties to be sure! David and Dante both loved to ride, and even though the weather was wretchedly cold, they managed to get a ride in nearly every day! The holidays passed quickly, with Dante returning to Florida.

David, Felicity, and Olivia followed Dante's baseball career closely. If they weren't watching baseball on TV, they were listening to it on the radio. David and Kenshin flew to Pittsburgh one weekend to watch a game. On another weekend David and Felicity flew to Los Angeles with Olivia and Marlene. At that time, they saw Dante play and he joined them later for a few hours, out in Anaheim, to visit Disneyland.

Olivia had begun staying in town quite often at her friend Marlene's house while they completed assignments together. It was their last year of high school and they were trying to get "certain projects" finished. It wasn't until later that the Carringtons learned it was Marlene's older brother Scott, home from university over Christmas break, that had been an added attraction!

Scott was a great kid, just a few years older than Olivia. He would be graduating in a few months with a degree in law, and had already been offered a job with a prestigious law firm in the city. Scott had served the Lord since a small child, and was known by his family, friends, and peers as a young man who walked in integrity. He was well-liked and respected. He had known Olivia since childhood, and had loved her from afar. He was ready to make a name for himself, and would dearly love Olivia Carrington to be part of his future life.

When questioned about her future plans Olivia was vague and distant. She seemed to have brushed away the future she had contemplated when she was younger. David and Felicity had often discussed with Olivia the possibility of taking nurse's training, like her mother, or maybe becoming a school teacher, which as a young girl she had always wanted to become. But in the past year, she had not made any commitments for her future years.

Finally, when confronted by her parents one evening, Olivia reluctantly mentioned she was thinking of applying for a job at Eaton's, like her Aunt Merrin. Maybe she would become a buyer for the store, and do a bit of travelling. David looked away and Felicity tried to reason with her, emphasizing that an education was so imperative! "Look at me," she said, "nursing is a good career. I went back to work and was even able to pick my shifts. There will always be need for nurses!"

Flippantly, Olivia answered, "Nursing isn't for me. I don't like cleaning up other people's messes!"

"That reminds me," said David evenly and without irritation, "I am glad you brought that up, Olivia. I cleaned up a mess you made in Missoula. Do you remember that?" Before she could answer, David continued very sincerely without raising his voice, "I am not asking you for the money. I know you don't have it and I don't expect it, and that is alright, but think about it, Olivia. What about your future? Education is vital in today's world." But she didn't want to hear.

The months flowed by quickly, as time does, and by the end of May graduation was right around the corner. Dante called Olivia to see if she needed an escort, and she eagerly told him no, that she had a date. He knew it was Scott, but she would not admit it. He told her that he was hoping to get home for the graduation, and she hoped that he would. His life with the team was hectic, but he loved it! He travelled and played in many of the American states! He had to admit that he did love travelling and seeing new places.

David and Felicity were increasingly concerned about Olivia's lack of interest in her future. School would be finished in six weeks! They were aware of the mood swings. She definitely was not the same girl she once had been. After school she went up to her room. She did not come down until she was called for supper, and then she did not eat. There was no more sitting around the table and sharing the day's events. Instead, she would immediately clear the table, start the dishes, and then go back up to her room.

Felicity asked Wilma Price about Olivia's behaviour when she stayed with them. Wilma said she had certainly detected a difference in her, but couldn't seem to pin it down as to why or what it was. On several occasions Felicity took Olivia aside and asked what was wrong. What was bothering her? It wasn't until Mr. Stewart, the school principal, called Felicity to share his own concerns about Olivia that both parents sat her down and confronted her. They asked, "What are your plans at the end of June?"

When Olivia did not answer, Felicity shared with both David and Olivia that she knew a young girl who positively hated being told what to do. She did what was expected of her, but always on her own terms, the way she wanted to do it. She had a temper but she often could control it. She pretended to be obedient and smile, at the right times, always to hide what she felt inside. In her own way she wanted to be good, but she didn't want anyone to tell her to be good, or tease her in any way! She violently recoiled at any kind of teasing! As a very young girl, it seemed her main goal was to get away from her parents, so she could be free of any rules of correction or advice. She wanted to dictate her own affairs and make her own decisions.

Olivia, with a quizzical look on her face, asked her mom who she was referring to. "Do I know her?"

"Yes, Olivia, you know her very well. You are that little girl. That is how I see you, Olivia. Your attitude will always prevent you from entering into a relationship with God and with other people." There was silence. Olivia didn't like hearing this! Both parents seemed at a loss for words. What to say? She had never realized that her independent spirit prevented God from being able to say anything back to her! And right about then she didn't care if He ever did!

Realizing their deep concern, part of her wanted to run into their arms. She wanted to have her mom hug her while saying, as she had said so many times, "It will be alright, my Pet."

But she didn't run into her parents' arms. Instead, she stiffened her neck and mockingly recited the old cliché she often used, "Not to worry, parents; I have a few plans of my own!"

David was quick to respond, "That is exactly what we are worried about. You have plans, but we are not privy to them." Olivia just smiled a "crocodile smile" and walked away!

Felicity was always concerned about depression. Her concern wasn't without foundation. Her father had been a good man, but he had suffered serious bouts of depression. When he was in this condition, he would lie on his bed and not talk to anyone. He could be very moody! Grace, her mother, had a tough life with Henry!

The situation with their daughter was both hurtful and discouraging for them, but they both knew the power of prayer. Nights would often find the Carringtons sitting in the lamplight, hands joined, praying for their skeptical daughter. It was so very obvious Olivia was hurting, and the change was so radical. They regularly stormed heaven with their prayers, and asked for a supernatural love to cover them as they dealt with her. She chose to be very sarcastic at times, and Felicity would repeatedly walk away teary-eyed. Just when Felicity would think she had gained ground with Olivia, and things were going well, a blow-up would ensue for such insignificant reasons.

It would be so easy as parents to give up, walk away, and let the chips fall where they may, but they both knew that God had a perfect plan for their little surprise bundle who had arrived without their even knowing she was coming. God had delicately formed Olivia within her mother's womb, and would not forsake her; that, they could rely on! She had been born a very fragile baby girl who later developed a weak immune system that caused her to rely on their help, and take life easy. This dependence had changed these past years. She no longer relied on her parents, and seemed to run into life with a gusto that was not completely authentic to her personality. But they were the parents, and they loved their daughter. They would trust God, and lean on Him. "He never fails!" David reminded his wife.

CHAPTER FIFTEEN

SECRET PLANS

WHEN DANTE ARRIVED HOME FOR HIS COUSIN'S GRADUATION weekend, he was shocked to find a sulky Olivia. The two cousins had always been close. At a very early age in her life she had declared, and he had proved, to be her champion!

One evening after David and Felicity had gone to bed, Olivia confided in Dante that her parents were always on her case. He asked, "Why? Why would they be, when they never were before?" She shrugged, indicating that she didn't know the reason. He urged her to talk. He knew his aunt and uncle very well, and they were the fairest-minded and most generous people he'd ever met.

He asked her outright what exactly had happened to put her at odds with them. She looked up at her handsome cousin and inquired, "Did they tell you about what happened last year in Missoula?" He replied that they had not. She was surprised, but she believed him. She then told him the story of meeting the girls, taking the car, getting into an accident, and David paying the court fine. She told him the cost of Grandma's car repairs, and how David had said she needed to be responsible to pay some of the money back. How was she supposed to do that? She abruptly burst into tears. Dante took his young cousin in his arms, and to her surprise began to pray that this spirit of anger would leave her. He prayed that she would forgive her parents and take responsibility for her actions, allowing God to take His place in her life. Although she didn't flinch or try to get out of his arms, she could see that Dante had grabbed hold of the "religious cure" and she just couldn't handle it anymore. He didn't release her. Instead, he quietly began to sing a song they had sung as children:

"In His time, In His time, He makes all things beautiful in His time. Lord, please show me every day, as You're teaching me your way, that You do just what You say, in Your time."

Letting her go he smiled and whispered in her ear, "Trust God, Livvy; He keeps His promises; they are worth waiting for." She smiled up into the dark black eyes, hoping to convince him that her intentions were to do just that, and wordlessly left the room. She had intended to confront him with her questions regarding his bank books and his acquired fortune, but it seemed as if Dante was on a forgiveness kick, probably at her parents' suggestion, she mused. Once more, and very deliberately, she stuffed the growing bitterness down inside and pasted on a Happy Face!

School was over now for Olivia and Marlene, and the future lay before them. Marlene was having problems with her legs, because of the polio she had suffered when she was ten years old. Her doctor felt she required a few weeks of daily physiotherapy, so after talking it over with the Carringtons, it was decided that the girls might rent a small apartment together in Moose Jaw. They would share the expenses. Olivia would find work, and Marlene would continue her therapy at the local hospital. They were thrilled to be together, and both families came up with all the furniture they would need plus a supply of groceries that would seemingly last a lifetime! This was not what David and Felicity would have chosen for Olivia, but short of forcing her, which would have been impossible, they agreed to the plan. They remained grateful that Olivia had a good friend in Marlene.

Olivia applied at Eaton's and was hired immediately in the shoe department. After three days, she shared with Marlene that she despised helping people with shoes, and didn't want to work there. Marlene advised her that she had better stick it out for a while, as quitting three days after starting a new job would not look good on her resume. She struggled on, not liking it, and her attitude was soon brought to the attention of the department manager. After talking with Olivia, he told her there was a position opening up in the jewellery department, and she could apply for that. Would she like that better? She did, and so she was hired. She loved working in this department, and she drooled over the jewellery and the locked display of diamonds. She soon discovered, as espoused by the well-to-do women who shopped for diamonds, that "diamonds are a girl's best friend". It wasn't long before she had an expensive watch on layaway, along with a delicate fourteen-carat gold chain. She began to love nice things! They made her feel good… for a while.

Scott Price had moved to Moose Jaw after getting his degree in law, and he had started his new position at a local law firm. He spent most evenings visiting with Marlene and Olivia. Taking them out to the Exchange Café for Chinese food was often on the agenda. Marlene, whose health had improved, decided that she would commence her training to become a physical therapist. Soon, she would be moving to Saskatoon!

Marlene hugged Olivia close as she said goodbye. Marlene was leaving for university in Saskatoon, and she would miss her best friend. Olivia had been a lifeline for her these past few weeks, and she felt badly leaving her alone in the small apartment. She hoped she would be able to find a roommate fairly soon, to help with the expenses. She noted that Olivia didn't seem at all concerned, and so it was with joy she hugged her and boarded the Greyhound bus that would take her to Saskatoon and her new life.

Somewhere in these weeks of decision-making and transitions, Scott and Olivia started seeing each other. As the saying goes, they "fell in love" and become secretly engaged! He presented her with a diamond ring that had cost him nearly all of his savings. She was pleased to be engaged, and she did love him, but she found herself, of all things, disappointed in the size of the diamond. Without mentioning a word to him, she took the ring to work to have it sized, and to have the diamond upgraded to a carat! She would use the three hundred American dollars from her grandmother to replace the original diamond with a one-carat stone. She was delighted when the ring was returned. She glowed with approval as she showed it to Scott, who smiled and wasn't even aware of the change. She didn't elaborate. As they sat eyeing the ring on her finger, he asked her when they might consider getting married. He had a good job, and his grandma's house in Moose Jaw would one day be his. Olivia thought of the beautiful home on Main Street that belonged to Grandma Price. She had been to it many times with Marlene when they were younger. Furnished with numerous antiques, a spiral oak staircase up to the second floor, large bay windows, and a huge backyard, it was a heritage home of rare splendour. "Would you be able to get your grandma's house soon?" she asked.

He replied, "She promised that if I graduated and became a lawyer, she would give me the house... lock, stock, and barrel, and she would move into a retirement place. But Grandma isn't ready for a retirement home yet!"

Olivia Carrington saw a good thing! She quietly and deftly unfolded her plans to Scott, and he, being so infatuated with her, reciprocated, without consulting his family, or hers! She wanted to elope! "It would be exciting, wouldn't it? Let's just drive down across the border for the weekend." They began making their plans, promising secrecy in regards to both of their families.

Olivia and Scott planned their getaway for the first week in August. Never once did she vacillate in the plans they had made. Several times Scott had brought up the fact that their parents might be upset, but Olivia talked him out of that. She reassured him that her parents had spent a lot of money on her in regards to the accident in Missoula last year, and she didn't want to burden them with the expense of a wedding. Scott shook his head in puzzlement, but deferred to Olivia's delight in the "secrecy" of it all. It was easier to pull off than she thought it would be. Living in Moose Jaw, she wasn't always expected to come home to the farm every weekend, so a quick phone call to her mother explaining that she had plans in the city was satisfactory.

On the following Tuesday afternoon, the Carringtons noticed Scott's new car pull into the yard, and out hopped the two of them. Felicity was excited. She was ready to serve David a chicken dinner, with all the trimmings, so she quickly ran to the cupboard to grab two more place settings before the children came inside. Calling David, she ran out to hug her beautiful daughter. Instantly, she knew there was something up! David arrived and grabbed Olivia in a bear hug, and when he finally put her down, Olivia simply and gracefully extended her left hand to show her sparkling diamond ring, now joined with a wide band of gold. For a moment Felicity could not concentrate on the picture presenting itself before them. Her head began to spin. She thought she saw a wedding ring on Olivia hand. And was Olivia beaming from ear to ear? Was Scott also beaming, for that matter? Wonderful, steady, sweet, stable, respectful Scott Price! What had they done???

Scott spoke first, and explained that they had gone to Minot, North Dakota and gotten married. They were married in a small church there, and he hoped the Carringtons wouldn't have a problem with that. He assured them his mother would be alright with it. David and Felicity invited them to sit down. Both of them had to compose their emotions. Whatever was done, was done. It could not be undone! Was it a terrible mistake, or was this God's surprising plan? Both of them were thinking of Olivia. She had challenged them from the day she arrived, and had continued to challenge them throughout her eighteen years — especially these last couple of years. There were some uncomfortable moments as both parents realized the finality of the children's actions. Before they had time to voice their opinions, whatever they may be, a knock was sounded on the door, and Kenshin, Eiko, and the girls appeared carrying a large two-layer chocolate cake and ice cream. Kenshin immediately knew that they had interrupted a "family moment", and he subtly tried to move his family back out the door, but eager Olivia grabbed him by the arms and waved them all into the living room. For the second time, she stretched out her hand to show off the large sparkling diamond on her finger. Ami and Mai were the first to compliment the young couple. They grabbed Olivia and hugged her. They were both acquainted with Scott, and tentatively gave him a hug as well. Cake in hand, Eiko came to the rescue of what could have been an awkward moment. Offering the cake to Felicity she also embraced Olivia. Anticipation as well as celebration was definitely in the air. Four more plates were added to the table and the Akiras joined them for dinner.

    David and Felicity stole into the kitchen to prepare coffee and take a moment to contemplate the circumstances that had suddenly befallen them. They could hear Olivia extolling the virtues of her new husband, and in all honesty, they were in total agreement. They were fond of Scott, although they didn't know him that well, as he was older than Olivia. He most certainly had the respect of their small community, and seemed to be held in high esteem by all who knew him. If they had chosen a husband for their daughter, Scott might have been at the top of their list; however, they hadn't even considered this. She was young, and very immature, in their view. She was loved unconditionally, but nevertheless, they were concerned by her recent aggression. Picking up a tray of cups, David glanced at his wife. With deep emotion, using his pet name for her, he said, "Fel, this is a time where love must conquer all. Let's embrace them and hopefully at some point in time, we will be able to bridge this gap with Olivia." They entered the room, and cake and congratulations became the focus of the evening!

It was a very different story when the newlyweds visited Wilma Price with their news. She was extremely upset with her son's decision. She had nothing personal against Olivia, she said, but he had just started a new job, and wasn't ready, in her estimation, to have the responsibility of a wife and home. Why did they choose to run away and keep it a secret? They should have waited, shared their news with the families, and had a family wedding. Where would they live, and how would this affect her son's new job? She was disappointed, and the more they talked, the more anxious she became.

Scott reminded his mother of the promise Grandma Price had made to him as a young boy. No one in the family had yet earned a university degree, and if Scott were to do so, her beautiful home, along with all the furnishings, and everything in it, would be given to him, lock, stock, and barrel! "Don't you remember that promise, Mom? Couldn't we live there?" he asked. She explained to her son that his grandma would keep her promise, but it wouldn't come into effect until Grandma made that decision, and for now, she was managing quite alright, and still able to benefit being in her own place.

Both Scott and Olivia lowered their eyes to the floor as Wilma continued voicing her opinion that eloping and not having a wedding was selfish on both their parts. They both had family to consider; why would they have done this? Scott immediately regretted the position they had placed their families in.

Olivia, on the other hand, felt an immediate reaction to her new mother-in-law. She would not let her win this argument, nor would she allow her to treat them with such disrespect. She looked Wilma in the eye, and declared in a childish, but somewhat superior tone, that she didn't like her tone of voice, nor did she like hearing her husband of three days bombarded with Wilma's irate opinions. She was not going to stand idly by while someone berated her husband! She went doggedly on, telling Wilma that this was their business, and furthermore, they weren't here to ask for advice, but to announce their marriage. Wilma was quick and forthright to tell Olivia that she wasn't just "someone"; she was Scott's mother, and now Olivia's mother-in-law!

Scott and Olivia both declined the coffee and lunch that Wilma offered.

As they drove back to the city, Olivia again asked Scott about moving into Grandma Price's house. He looked at her incredulously, as if to say, "What part of my mother's tirade didn't you understand? The house will not be available until Grandma is ready to give it up. No more discussion on that issue, please!" Olivia was quiet, she pouted, she was miserable, she was mad, but she would see what she might do about it all! She liked her own way!

On Wednesday morning Olivia returned to her position in the jewellery department at Eaton's only to find a younger part-time girl behind the jewellery counter, with a message for Olivia to report to the manager's office. She did so, and Mr. Brand promptly presented her with a "pink slip" informing her of immediate dismissal. When she asked why, Mr. Brand informed her that she had taken the long weekend off, along with the rest of the staff, but had failed to show up for work on Tuesday morning. She hadn't informed anyone why, nor had she given the department a chance to bring in a replacement. Olivia assured Mr. Brand that she had called one of her friends in the ladies' department, and that she had asked her friend to relay the message to him that she wouldn't be back to work until Wednesday morning. Obviously, the message was never relayed! He told Olivia her actions were inappropriate, inconsiderate, and immature. If she had needed an extra day off for a valid reason, then it was her personal responsibility to call him, and not rely on someone else. Her request for him to reconsider his decision was answered by a very firm and unyielding no. She was being dismissed... let go... fired, in no uncertain terms. As she was going out the door, he requested very clearly that she clear up her charge account of over four hundred dollars still owing on the one-carat diamond, an expensive watch, and a very expensive gold chain! She was horrified and astounded by this turn of events, and spoke in defence of herself, but it was to no avail. The decision was final. Mr. Brand knew Olivia from her time in the shoe department, and considered her unreliable and temperamental.

It was an angry and cynical young woman who returned to the small, cramped apartment shortly after nine o'clock on that Wednesday morning. It was strange that when she and Marlene had occupied it, there seemed to be plenty of room, but ever since last week, when Scott had moved all of his clothes, books, hockey equipment, guitar, and several boxes of "stuff", there was hardly a place to sit down. Her thoughts revolved around the four hundred dollars she owed to the store, and the fact that Scott knew nothing about her changing the size and carat of the ring he had given her. As she looked at the outsized shimmering diamond now, it didn't seem to be as extremely important as it had seemed a few weeks before. She had not even worn the gold chain yet! She had expected to pay back a little every week, out of her own cheque, but now there would be no more cheques. She sat down and sighed resolutely. She would look for another job! "That might not be so easy," she thought. Olivia had certain boxed in criteria of what she was prepared to do. She most certainly was not going to work in a restaurant and serve meals, nor would she consider working in the kitchen or housekeeping at either one of the hospitals, so what was left? And, how would she tell Scott about the money she owed to Eaton's and the foolishness of changing and upgrading the diamond ring he had given her?

CHAPTER SIXTEEN

CERTAIN ADJUSTMENTS

IT WASN'T LONG BEFORE WORD SPREAD THROUGHOUT THE LITTLE community of the marriage in Minot, and a Bridal shower was held for Olivia. Grandmother Price and Marlene joined Olivia, Wilma, and Felicity at the head table as honoured guests. Various opinions probably existed, but were never voiced. The newlyweds received blankets, pillows, cream and sugar sets, pots and pans, tablecloths, lamps, ornaments, vases, china, various pieces of crystal, and silverware; cards with envelopes containing cheques and cash; and well-meaning congratulations! Both Wilma and Felicity smiled, but one might have wondered at what the two mothers were thinking. Olivia was on cloud nine that night. She appeared the lively recipient, and opened each gift with anticipation and excitement. She came across as wound up and excited. To the guests she gave the impression of a typical young bride, but to her mother-in-law, something was grossly exaggerated in this young woman.

Later, after the guests had departed and the gifts were being packed in their car for transport back to Moose Jaw, Olivia approached Wilma, who had a look of apprehension on her face. She proceeded to tell her new mother-in-law that she had had a long visit with Grandmother Price the day before, and Grandmother had shared her intention of moving from her Main Street house into a seniors' facility. The house would be turned over to Scott as soon as these plans could be arranged. Wilma was astounded. Juliana Price had always been a stalwart friend and confidant over the years. Wilma's husband, Harold Price, after struggling through eight years in the sanatorium at Fort Qu'Appelle due to acute tuberculosis, had died ten years ago. Wilma was left raising the three children by herself. Juliana Price was her deliverance, so to speak. Juliana's support and confidence were essential for the young mother to face the difficulties her situation presented. It was through Juliana's witness and strong faith in Christ that Wilma first heard about the gift of salvation. It was at her own kitchen table that Juliana led her daughter-in-law to the Lord, and opened up a new way of living and believing. When Harold Price passed away, it was once again Juliana who stepped in and took care of all the financial arrangements. Juliana had been instrumental in acquiring the position of postmistress for her. They were close friends and kept in contact regularly. Why hadn't Mother Price discussed this most important decision with her? She had never mentioned a word of this to Wilma in their conversations, and they got together every couple of weeks. Taking her son aside that evening, Wilma asked him about this development, and was told the same story by Scott. Grandma had told Olivia that arrangements were to be made soon, and he too was eager to move into the big house on Main Street!! A talk with Juliana would be on Wilma's "to do list", but tonight was not the time for that.

Olivia was pleasant and cooperative with Felicity that evening. Marlene was home, and with so many friends around congratulating and visiting with her, there was no time to discuss any of the details in regard to the upcoming move. She smiled and hugged her mother for the first time in almost two years. Even though the circumstances surrounding the evening were tense, Felicity was thrilled to hold her daughter close, and silently asked the Lord for His direction in Olivia's life.

Wilma made a trip to the city the next evening to see Juliana. She made no attempt at small talk, but got right to the point: "Have you been thinking of moving? Olivia mentioned you shared this with her. Is this true, Juliana?"

Juliana's face gave no reflection of what she might be thinking. "Why do you ask?" she smiled. "Did the children tell you what I was planning?"

"Olivia told me your plans, Juliana, and if they are your plans, that is fine with me, but if you are influenced at all by their circumstances, please don't consider making such a move; they are young, and have their whole lives ahead of them. This is your home, and you are comfortable here. You love this home, and you have never mentioned to me a desire to leave." A look of bewilderment masked Juliana's face for a brief instant, and then her expression quickly changed to one of confidence. With a smile, she told Wilma the stairs to the second floor were giving her trouble, and she did think it might be time for a move. Wilma immediately suggested that instead of moving, why didn't she just move her bedroom down to the main floor? For instance, the den or the library would work perfectly. Juliana just smiled, and said she had made up her mind. She was trying to convince Wilma this was her desire and her wish, but to a large degree, Wilma did not believe her. After some tea and a visit, Wilma prepared to leave Juliana's home. She asked her to pray before making a final decision. Juliana gracefully said she had prayed, and would pray some more. Putting her arms around her mother-in-law, and hugging her, Wilma was aware of the fragile bones, and she wondered again if it really was her desire to move, or if Olivia had influenced her to come to this decision. Getting in her car, she decided she would stop and listen to what Scott and Olivia had to say about this. She would discuss this with both of them. On the drive to their apartment she rehearsed what she might ask, but to her bitter disappointment, they were not home. She actually waited in front of the apartment for nearly forty-five minutes, and when they didn't return, she started her car, and left for home.

She too, was a praying mother, and she fervently prayed that her suspicions of Olivia were totally mistaken. She highly respected David and Felicity Carrington. She had known Olivia as a youngster. She was her daughter's best friend; the two girls had grown up together. She loved Olivia. But Olivia had changed, and Wilma was concerned that the influence she had over her son was not so good! Perplexed and feeling totally judgmental, she began to cry.

Several days later, a call from Juliana confirmed that there would be a move, and soon! She had already called her lawyer to transfer the deed of the house to Scott and Olivia. Juliana realized she would not be able to take all of her treasured furniture with her, and offered Wilma the large provincial red cherrywood bedroom suite in the upstairs guest room that she had always admired, and often slept in while visiting Juliana. It consisted of a canopied bed, dresser and mirror, high chest of drawers, and two matching night tables. Wilma smiled at the thought of it fitting into one of her small bedrooms. She might get the bed in, but the rest of the pieces would have to go in another room. She declined the generous offer, and said, "No, please give it to the children. Hopefully they will appreciate it."

But Juliana dearly wanted Wilma to have something from her home. She then offered Wilma the bevelled glass china cabinet that contained so many gorgeous china tea cups, some of which had been gifts to Juliana from Wilma herself. "Would you like that?" she asked.

"Yes, that would be a wonderful addition in my living room, and a good reminder of the many cups of tea we have shared while discussing many of life's issues and our walk with the Lord over the years." Wilma was thrilled to be the recipient of such a beautiful gift, and had the perfect place for it in her living room.

Olivia was home alone the next morning when the phone rang. After asking to speak with Olivia Carrington, Eaton's Credit office informed her of her outstanding bill of over four hundred dollars.

Her account was overdue; no payments had been made. As she was no longer employed by the Eaton Company, they would like the account cleared, and if it wasn't taken care of in fifteen days, Eaton's would be taking action against her. She promised the money would be there in the next few days and she asked them to please not send a letter to her husband. After some planning and conniving, she formed her plan!

The next afternoon, she dressed in a new outfit and visited Scott's office in the prestigious law offices of Ryan, Mackey, and Burns on the third floor of the Stafford Building. She had never been to his office, and she didn't have an appointment. Somewhat nervously, she opened the double doors of the reception area to see the most beautiful décor. Deep jade green walls were accented with cream-coloured wallpaper and wainscoting, venetian blinds covered some of the windows, large leafy plants filled the corners, and several wine-coloured velvet loveseats gave a place for waiting clients to sit in comfort. The carpet on the floor was a dark grey plush, which your feet couldn't help but sink into as you walked. A receptionist showed Olivia into Scott's office. He ushered her in and quickly shut the door. Not hesitating to embrace her, he kissed her passionately on the lips. He motioned for her to have a seat. He was pleased she had finally come to see him at his office. Looking around the room, she decided it was a nice office. It was not nearly as roomy as she thought it might be, but nevertheless, it was very well-decorated with a window facing Fairford Street. "It could be bigger," she mentioned, and he laughed, saying that in a few months it probably would be!

After some light talk, he asked her why she was there. "Any particular reason?" She answered that she had found a painter who would be willing to paint the new house for only four hundred dollars, and he could start tomorrow. Scott shook his head. "Olivia, Grandma isn't moving out till Friday. We can't paint while she is there." She went on to explain that she needed one hundred dollars to make a down payment and to purchase the paint, and the painter could wait till the weekend. Scott shook his head in disagreement. He had planned on hiring a couple of guys he knew. She thought quickly, and replied that because she didn't know them, and she would be in the house while the painting was going on, she wanted to feel comfortable. She would feel comfortable with Daniel Brandt, who had been recommended by his grandma's new neighbour Rose Ireland, and Olivia wanted him. Scott acquiesced to her plans, saying it would be alright with him. He didn't have time to oversee the painting anyway, so it could be Olivia's project. Without hesitation, Scott reached into his pocket and counted out five twenty-dollar bills. Before leaving, she thanked him for the money. He kissed her again, promising to meet her for supper at their favourite Chinese restaurant, The Exchange Café, at six p.m.

With Grandma's three hundred, and one hundred from Scott, she marched into the Eaton's credit office and paid off her account, telling the woman in the office that the Price family would be customers no longer. Leaving the office, she strolled to the main floor where she had previously worked in the jewellery department. She was still mesmerized with the diamonds, the gold chain jewellery, and various other pieces. She lifted her head high. She was Mrs. Scott Price now, and one day she would have no problem owning expensive good jewellery, and it wouldn't be purchased from a department store either!!!

CHAPTER SEVENTEEN

HOME FROM THE DODGERS

On a warm spring morning Felicity heard the phone ringing, but before she could answer it, David picked up. For a moment, she heard that sense of inquiry in his voice, and her thoughts automatically ran to Dante. Had something happened to him? After a few minutes, David hung up the phone to tell her it was Steophano Castrinni, letting them know that Michaelo, Dante's grandfather, had passed away peacefully in his sleep. He was eighty-seven years old. David would relay this message to Dante.

Dante got up for the second time that night, chipped some ice, and made an ice pack to cover his left arm and elbow. He had pitched two consecutive games in Cincinnati, beating the Braves 4-1 and belting in a home run, but the thrill of the game, and there certainly was that, didn't compare to the suffering he was experiencing at the present time. Doc Wharton, the team's physician, had told the young pitcher that without an X-ray he couldn't assess the damage, but he was pretty sure Dante had torn a ligament in his left arm, and no doubt his pitching days were numbered. Sad to say, but that's life in the big leagues!

When he received the call from Uncle David that his grandfather Michaelo had recently passed away, it was hard for Dante to define his feelings. He did remember seeing an old picture of his grandparents holding him as a baby, at three months old. Other than that, his memories all came from various recollections his aunt and uncle had shared with him. Always positive!

As he lay back down in bed, he began to pull up whatever memories he had of his parents… there were none, really. He had photos, but he did not personally remember them! He had often reminisced with Uncle David about his father, Nicholas Castrinni, whom David and Felicity thought so highly of; his parents' one and only visit to the farm; and the accident that took their lives. They rejoiced together in the fact that the Castrinnis had accepted the Lord as their Saviour, and because of that, one day there would be a great reunion. Until then, he wanted to make his aunt and uncle proud of him.

Lately he had found himself wondering about his family in Italy. They had sent the monthly cheques, and had even flown to Canada to take him to Italy. What were they like? Why had his father left Italy at such a young age?

David and Felicity had been very careful to keep their true feelings from Dante, but he was a wise young man, and could assess situations for himself. Nevertheless, they were his father's family, his Italian family! Maybe if he couldn't play ball, he would go to Italy and meet them. Yes, maybe he would. He could surely afford the trip. He had made good money from the Dodgers, and had never touched his inheritance. Actually, he had never bothered much about the inheritance. He really didn't know just how much money there was, but he realized he was the owner of the Villa Val di Pesa, and tried to imagine what that would look like. Yes, a trip to Italy in the upcoming off-season might happen! Until then, he would rest his arm and pray that his baseball career would not end prematurely. He truly loved baseball, and enjoyed the camaraderie of the players, and definitely loved the travelling. However, he did wonder what were God's plans and purposes for his career, and for his Italian family, but for now, he would leave this up to God.

Dante was as faithful as he could be about going to church, but when on the road, he did what the team did. He played baseball. He tried to make up for it by spending time reading the Bible and in prayer, and he was unconsciously being drawn closer to the Master in such a way that it wouldn't be such a hard thing for him to lay baseball down, and let God choose!

He had been surprised at Olivia's sudden wedding to Scott Price. He had called home immediately after receiving the news! He had shopped long and hard before deciding on a wedding gift for his cousin. While passing by a jewellery store in New York, he saw a sign that advertised Murano glass, made in Italy. He remembered that his mother had flown to Italy as a young girl to buy Murano glass for the Timothy Eaton Company in Toronto, and it was there she had met Nicholas Castrinni, his father. He purchased a glass and sliver-plated flared bowl, and matching candlesticks. It cost him well over a month's salary, but he knew Olivia would appreciate the thought behind the gift. She liked "nice" things!

He wished his cousin well and prayed for her often. She was like a sister to him, and he was aware and concerned in regards to the recent change in her. After he had left home she had changed and become so disrespectful to David and Felicity. Maybe now that she was a married woman, things would change for the better. He hoped so.

The next two years after Olivia's surprise wedding passed quickly for Dante. She had written a couple of times. He always remembered her birthday, and she remembered his! He wasn't much for writing letters, so he usually called her and would talk to Scott also. She was busy redecorating the house that Grandma Price had given them, and this kept her busy.

While in the playoffs in Los Angeles, Dante struggled with immeasurable pain. In a game between the Dodgers and San Francisco Giants, he came close to passing out, but still managed to keep up his batting average and pitches! But the inevitable happened, and not in the way he expected. A ball hit him in the elbow. He heard the sound of shattering bone, and immediately felt the excruciating pain, then nothing... unconsciousness crept in. After being taken to the hospital, surgeons advised immediate surgery to remove the shattered bone. Hopefully his arm would heal, and he could still play some ball. After various consultations with surgeons, he underwent the required surgery. A few months later, still struggling after every game, he decided he would hang up his cleats and leave with a good record. He had pitched an outstanding career, but it was still a blue day when he said goodbye to the team.

As he flew into Toronto, he decided he would spend some time in the city of his birth, and the city his parents had loved so much. During the flight, he was seated next to an older gentleman who immediately engaged Dante in an animated and interesting conversation. He spoke in what Dante believed to be an Italian accent. Over the course of their conversation his fellow passenger soon realized the young man seated next to him was Dante Castrinni, the left-handed pitcher for the Dodgers. His baseball enthusiasm had Dante confessing he had always wanted to pitch for the Yankees. The old man laughed and confessed that he too loved the New York Yankees, and was an avid fan. His name was Paolo Salvatore Russo, from Milan, Italy. He was seventy-two years old and had travelled to Miami, Florida, to meet his firstborn grandson. Paolo was now returning to Milan, where he had worked for many years in the La Scala Opera House. He had started out as a janitor, then was promoted to messenger, then to doorman, then to ticket taker, and at present he was a host at night and a guide by day. He would be retiring in one year! As Dante then shared the story of his parents and his relatives who were still living in Florence, and his plans of visiting Italy in the near future, a firm bond was made with a promise to visit.

After spending two nights in Toronto, Dante flew into Regina, where he was shocked at the welcoming committee. David, Felicity, Kenshin, Eiko, the twins, and many fans were outside on the tarmac when he landed.

He hugged Uncle David and realized how good it felt to have his uncle's arms around him again. Family was important. On the drive home, amidst Felicity's questions, he thought about another family… the family in Italy… his family in Italy. For the first time in his twenty-two years, he knew this was the time to meet them, and investigate his background. He shared his idea with his aunt and uncle, and they also felt this was the right time. His arm was healing and the constant pain was gone, but there was still a weakness. He decided he would first spend some quality time with his aunt and uncle, Kenshin and his family, and Scott and Olivia. He would renew relationships with his schoolmates, and relax for a time. This announcement was greatly received by the family. They had missed Dante, and were excited to have him around for a while.

Michael Gallo, the family lawyer, had recently moved to Regina. He had kept abreast of Dante's baseball career, and had become a family friend to David and Felicity over the years. When he met with Dante to bring him up-to-date on his financial holdings, Dante was for the first time very attentive to the amount of his wealth. He remembered Uncle David showing him the two bank books and the deed to the Villa, along with the other investments, but honestly, at that time, his mind had been on baseball and his upcoming adventure, and so he really hadn't considered the amount. Now, the realization overwhelmed him, and the idea of holding the deed to the Villa Val di Pesa opened a new door. He was now free to seek God's advice as to what his future might hold.

Uncle David was in the midst of buying a herd of Thoroughbred horses from Lexington, Kentucky, and he quickly convinced Dante to return to Kentucky with him to pick out the horses. They left with high hopes of spending time together and enjoying their shared love of the great runners. It would be interesting to visit the many farms and choose those horses with well-chiselled heads, long necks, and high withers that are classified amongst the "hot-blooded breeds". Although David wasn't interested in the racing as much as the breeding, he loved the look of a "good horse". On the first day at Covington Farms, David purchased three beauties: Mexican Dude, Native Dancer, and Uncle Mo. Dante felt drawn to a young filly named Four Winds, and so Uncle David included her in the day's purchases. David and Dante flew back to Regina satisfied with their choices, and with having spent time with each other.

David sensed that Dante had "Italy" on his mind, and felt the young man would be leaving soon to explore his birthright. He wasn't wrong. A few days after returning home from Kentucky, Dante mentioned his plans to fly to Italy and meet his father's family. He immediately wrote to Paolo Russo, the older gentleman he had met on the plane from Florida, and decided to fly into Milan and travel the country from there. Paolo returned a letter quickly, saying he would be thrilled to meet Dante and show him around. His ticket was purchased. In two weeks he would leave for Italy and "his family reunion".

Time was spent with David and Felicity. Dante and Uncle David spent hours riding two of the Thoroughbreds that had been purchased. Dante rode Four Winds and Uncle David rode Mexican Dude. Dante valued every minute spent with his uncle. He also loved hearing Aunt Felicity tell the story of his parents' trip out to the prairies, even though he was too small to remember. Felicity recalled the party they had with the neighbours and again told Dante how his father Nicholas had left money for the purchase of a piano for Myrna. She talked about Dante's time in the hospital, lonely and not understanding where his parents were, not knowing what had happened. He could not remember this. Nor did he remember meeting Uncle Steophano or his two aunties.

Kenshin carefully attended to the farm, giving David lots of time to spend with Dante and Felicity. Scott and Olivia spent time visiting at the farm, but Olivia couldn't understand Dante's desire to meet the family that had never had anything to do with him. She did remember her parents telling how three of the family had come to the farm, shortly after Dante left for training camp, with hopes of taking Dante back to Italy, but she had never personally met them.

CHAPTER EIGHTEEN

ITALY AND THE VILLA

So many thoughts swirled through Dante's mind as Flight 1612 Air Italia left the ground from Toronto Pearson Airport. Anticipation mixed with uneasiness caused Dante to close his eyes, lay back, and reflect over the past twenty-three years of his life. He wondered what might be before him! He looked forward to seeing Paolo Russo and touring the city of Milan before heading out to Florence and the family. Uncle Steophano, as far as he knew, was still in residence with Grandma Gaetane in Florence. Grandfather had passed away over two years ago, when Dante was in the playoffs. He hadn't heard about his death until a month after the passing. He wondered what the family was like. Would they be pleased to meet Him? There had never been any interaction between Dante and his Italian family in all these years. He thought maybe he should have called them first, telling them about his arrival, but it was too late now. He was on his way!

From Toronto he flew directly into Milan, where he stayed overnight. He spent the morning just walking around the streets.

He stopped and had coffee at an outside café, and remembered the story of his mother sitting at an outside café in Venice all those years ago when Nicholas Castrinni first saw her. At noon he reserved a small table at the L'Antico Ristorante located in the heart of Milan's historic centre where Paolo Russo met him for lunch. Paolo looked well and hugged Dante as if he were a long-lost relative!! They talked about his baseball and the fact that Dante had decided to end his career. Paolo was quick to say he thought there was a greater plan for Dante here in Italy. Milan was a beautiful city, famous for its fashion houses and upscale shops, and timeless for its famous musicals — particularly opera. They were close to the Teatro alla Scala where Paolo Russo still worked, and he was able to take Dante on an inside tour of La Scala. Dante was absolutely enthralled at the history and uniqueness of the ancient building. Paolo was invited to come out to the Villa and visit in a couple of months. After making some tentative plans, Dante flew into Venice. That evening he attended the symphony where his father had played so many years ago. He enjoyed it immensely, and was reminded again of his heritage and the gift his father had been given in playing the violin. Later he would take the train to Florence to meet his relatives, but first he decided to see the country of his ancestors. He would check out the Villa!

A few days later he rented a small car and drove in the direction of Florence, out in Tuscany, where the family lived.

After a few stops for taking pictures, he drove directly to the Villa Val di Pesa, which was situated about twenty-five kilometres from the main home in Florence. He had previously contacted the caretakers in regards to his arrival, asking them not to inform the Castrinni family of his coming.

The drive to the Villa was scenic and picturesque, to say the least! He drove off the main highway and up a sloping gravel road for about a mile before the Villa came into view. He hadn't really known what to expect, but he was not in any way disappointed from this distance. The road was bordered on either side by tall and stately Italian cypress trees. They were as green as green could be. And, then, there it was: The Villa Val di Pesa! His villa! He could see immediately that beyond the need for paint and some refurbishing, the aged beauty of his father's family summer home was well cared for. Dante was thrilled at the prospect of it belonging to him.

He was met in the driveway by an elderly couple who introduced themselves as Aldo Vespone and his wife Doneta. They had been the gardener and housekeeper at the Villa for many years. The two of them lived in a comfortable suite of rooms over the garage. They explained that even though the family didn't use the Villa now, they had been kept on to maintain it.

Doneta recalled Nicholas as a young boy. She also remembered him as a young man, when he had brought Merrin and the tiny baby over for a visit in the spring of 1940. She commented on how much Dante resembled his father.

Aunt Felicity had done her best to describe the Villa to him by remembering things that his father had shared with her years before, but in no way did his aunt's description relate to what Dante saw before him. Up close, the Villa itself represented a living connection to his parents, and to his Italian heritage! Aldo excitedly began describing the property. It had been built by Umberto Ferrara, Dante's great grandfather, in 1890, and given to his daughter Gaetane at her marriage to Michaelo Castrinni. It covered well over three hundred hectares of dark rich soil, and included a grape vineyard and a smaller olive grove, the winery, and a large vegetable and flower garden. The garden, in full bloom, was awash with vibrant reds, yellows, and purples. An abundant variety of trees surrounded the Villa.

Many trees around the house were in good shape and had been well looked after, but looking farther to the outskirts, he could see the remnants of grape vines that looked gnarled and totally neglected. Off to the east was a covered veranda and a large swimming pool, empty of water and full of brightly coloured leaves. He remembered the stories of the young Castrinni children spending so many hours by the pool. There were stables that at one time had housed eight horses. This caught Dante's eye right away! He thought of Four Winds, the Kentucky Thoroughbred that Uncle David had recently bought for him. There was a three-car garage that had been recently shingled and painted. He noticed that the grass around the Villa was green and mowed short. Pails of bright red geraniums and another unfamiliar flower had been placed every five or six feet around the front and the back of the house. The main house was massive in comparison to what he had imagined! After all, this had been their summer house and they had five children. The outside walls of the main house were faded yellow, and the windows were shuttered in what at one time would have been a deep burgundy red.

The roof was covered in faded red terracotta shingles that were in excellent condition, as far as he could see. A covered portico and patio with weathered outside furniture were still very welcoming as well as comfortable-looking. As he entered the house through the back kitchen door, he tried to imagine his grandparents, aunts, uncles, and their youngest brother, Nicholas, sitting around the huge wooden table. He admired the polished wooden floors and rugs; the marble countertops; a modern gas stove and refrigerator; and the ten-foot high ceilings! Next, Dante went up a narrow staircase to six bedrooms and a fairly modern bathroom. Most of the rooms were empty of any furniture except for one large room that he surmised to be the master bedroom, which had long red silk curtains and a canopy over the bed. No doubt this had been Grandmother Gaetane's room when she occupied the Villa. There were some wooden chairs, a small writing desk of fine cherrywood, and a lampstand with an opaque pearl shade.

On the main floor there was an enormous dining room, empty except for a small watercolour hanging on the wall. It had obviously been painted by one of the children. The large foyer and main sitting room were also empty of furniture, but the buffed and polished floors were a deep reddish-blond colour.

There were ornate sconces on the walls in the foyer and a heavy but delicately carved wooden door that led to the outside garden. Most of the many windows were tall, like the ceilings, and the sunlight pouring in gave the house a warm feeling. "This house is now my house! Mi casa!"

CHAPTER NINETEEN

MEETING THE FAMILY

IT WAS TIME TO MEET THE FAMILY! DID HE FEEL ANXIOUS? YES! Excited? Yes! He called the phone number Uncle David had given him, and waited for what seemed a lengthy time. Eight rings, nine rings, and just as he was about to hang up, a voice said, "Hello?" He determined at once this was Uncle Steophano and he quickly identified himself. There was another long pause, and the voice asked, in English, "Our boy?"

"Yes, this is Dante, and I am about ten minutes away from your place. Is it a good time to come over?"

It seemed Uncle Steophano was flabbergasted and couldn't get a reply out. Dante repeated himself. Then he heard a deep, throaty laugh, and an invitation, "Yes, come quickly." A taxi quickly deposited Dante in front of 133 Via Montalese. A very tall distinguished-looking man was waiting in the doorway with his arms outstretched, and a smile on his face. He embraced his young nephew, and tears ran down his face unabashedly. This was Uncle Steophano! His hug was strong and both arms encircled Dante, who felt genuinely connected to this far distant relative, even though he did not remember any personal contact. It seems blood had transcended time, and he knew this was family, come what may!

He was ushered into a dark foyer where he found it hard to really see his uncle's face. Then he was told in a hushed voice that Grandma was having her midday sleep, and when she woke up she would be overjoyed to see her only grandson. After entering the main room, Steophano immediately called his sister Elena to announce Dante's arrival, and excitement was in the air! She would call the rest of the family and most of them would come over to see Dante before too long!

So many questions were asked in the ensuing minutes that Dante felt his head spinning. Steophano, suddenly realizing he was bombarding the boy with too many questions all at once, laughed at himself. With an apology, he sat back and just looked at Dante with a wistful look on his face. He was either looking at his young brother Nicholas, or an exact replica of him! He was visibly shaken and wondered how his mother would react. She was not in good health. She was very frail and had no doubt been experiencing a form of dementia for the past year, but this would be a remarkable day for the whole of the Castrinni family. Dante had finally come home!

Out of nowhere coffee and a tray of pastries were brought out, and Dante and his uncle settled into a very large sitting room on the main floor.

Uncle Steophano was not that interested in his baseball career, but, "What are your plans for the future?" As of yet, Dante had not thought about the future, other than the opening up of the Villa and his plans to bring over Four Winds. He would take a long holiday! "What about the grape orchard?" asked Uncle Steophano. "Are you interested in bringing it back to life? And how many men will you be employing? Will you be living at the Villa? Are you interested in selling the Villa?" Questions, questions, questions! Dante didn't have time to answer before another one was asked. Again, Steophano realized his numerous eager questions were confounding Dante.

Apologizing again for his enthusiasm, he patted Dante on the back, and in Italian, welcomed him into the family with another massive hug!

"Welcome, sei cosi benvenuto." (Welcome to my home.) "Mio nipote giovana!" (My young nephew!) He seemed anxious to bring Dante up-to-date with an account of the family's past. He shared how years ago, he had purchased a business in Venezuela, and had planned to take up residence there. But when Nicholas had left so suddenly, he was required to stay in Italy and help with his parents and the winery. His partner in the venture quickly took over, and eventually the project collapsed. Uncle Steophano was left with nothing. The family's plan was always for Nicholas to continue with his music. He would play with the symphony, but also take over the main supervision of the winery. Both of his sisters were married to influential businessmen and were independently wealthy in their own rights. Mimi, the youngest daughter, had graduated from the University of Rome as a surgical veterinarian, and was presently in Jeddah, Saudi Arabia, working as head veterinarian to Prince El Amari. She looked after his prize Arabian racehorses. Aunt Mimi had only come home once, when her father died. Dante began to feel uncomfortable while his uncle was talking. Had his uncle held a grudge against Nicholas for all these years? Did he feel cheated that he had to stay home and care for his parents? Was the whole family disappointed in his father? But as Steophano talked, Dante realized there was no bitterness or animosity in his voice. He was just telling Dante his viewpoint regarding the past. Suddenly, Steophano again looked at his young nephew, and with a raising of his hands, apologized at his outburst. He threw his arms once again around Dante, saying, "I'm so glad you are here. Mama will be so excited. Thank you for coming." Dante identified no tension or stiffness in his uncle, only a great sense of relief. Steophano did eventually ask about his baseball career. He seemed genuinely disappointed that he had left because of an injury, and was quick to assure Dante there were excellent physicians in Rome. He would be glad to make arrangements for Dante to see one of them. His uncle meant well, but Dante knew his life was not in pro baseball anymore!

Regarding the house, Dante observed the splendour. Antiquated, yes, but with furniture of the finest construction. Delicate pieces mingled alongside heavy pieces to set an atmosphere of a home that was well-lived in and comfortable. Potted palms and bowls of fresh verena and stephanotis were amply situated around the room. Oil paintings covered the walls, along with ornate mirrors and lamps. Glassed-in bookshelves lined part of a wall, filled with what looked like very old books that Dante hoped he might look over one day. Tall, sparkling, and impressive floor-to-ceiling windows gave view to a well-manicured backyard that was bordered with tall Italian cypress and pines. Bordering the trees were different flowers of opulent colours. Such magnificence took his breath away!

They were discussing how Uncle David had invested in the horses, and Dante shared his desire to bring Four Winds over. Even in the intensity of their conversation, a thin frail voice was suddenly heard, "I'm ready!" His uncle quickly rose up from his chair and motioned for Dante to follow him. Up a long, carpeted staircase they went, all the time hearing Grandmother's voice repeating, "I'm ready." And there she was! Standing in an open door. What a beauty! Quite tall, slim, and well-dressed in a mauve-coloured pant suit, her silver hair had been cut in a stylish bob. Makeup and silver earrings adorned her, and she had a smile that lit up the room.

As Steophano moved Dante forward, she embraced the young man, crying softly, "Nicholas, my Nicholas." She held him tightly and spoke rapidly in Italian. Both Steophano and Dante realized, at the same time, that she had mistaken Dante for his father. Dante helplessly listened as Uncle Steophano tried explaining that this was her grandson Dante from Canada. But his efforts were to no avail; to her, this was definitely her long-awaited son, returned as she always thought he would.

An elevator brought them down to the main floor with Gaetane holding Dante's hand and looking at him questioningly, as neither one could communicate in the other's language. Grandma Gaetane seemed to be mesmerized as well as puzzled! Here was Nicholas, finally at home, and yet he didn't seem to grasp that it was her, and he expressed nothing that she could understand! It bothered Dante as well, as he was aware of her confusion, and he felt badly. He chided himself. He should have learned to converse in Italian, as she spoke not a word of English.

After a short time, Aunt Elena burst through the front door with her two daughters. There was hugging and kissing and tears, as she embraced her nephew! They spoke English, and he found himself becoming calmer as Aunt Elena introduced him to his cousins, Maria and Sophia. Both of them were a couple of years older than Dante. Sophia was an elementary teacher at a local school in Florence. Maria, the older daughter, was attending the university in Rome. Apparently, she and a quite a few of her friends had followed his career with the Dodgers! She was a sports fan and would soon be graduating as a physical therapist, specializing in top sports medicine. She was interested in all kinds of sports and especially the injuries that could be helped by her intervention, but, to be truthful, baseball was her favourite sport! Dante was surprised at Maria's enthusiasm for baseball. She eagerly told him about the history of baseball in Italy. The first game was played in 1884. After World War II the game increased in popularity when some of the U.S. soldiers taught the game to the local children. The first professional league was established in 1948. Maria told Dante that there were a few guys close by who had a small pick-up team, and her fiancé, Rom, was part of the team. It would be great for Dante to meet them all and he said he would look forward to that!

Aunt Elena bustled about, making sure everyone had enough to eat and drink. She kept glancing at her nephew thoughtfully, remembering the past encounters with the Carrington family. She realized, very shortly, that this was a good boy. He had been brought up well, and projected a keen interest in life's values and relationships! A boy to be proud of! Yes. The Carringtons had raised Dante well!

Within a very short time everyone began to realize that Grandma Gaetane was facing serious difficulty in her comprehension. She clearly presumed this was her son, Nicholas, who had finally come home! Steophano and Elena both assured Dante that he did look like his father. To complicate matters, Nicholas was Dante's age when he had died. How to handle this situation, they had no idea; Grandma's eyes never left Dante, but at the same time, deep confusion and bewilderment clouded her face. Dante sat down beside her, and placed his arms around her shoulders. She leaned into him, closed her eyes, and within minutes she was fast asleep! He silently asked the Lord for help in being able to connect with his grandmother, and that his sudden appearance would not upset or confuse her in any way. This completely overwhelmed Dante. This family he had never met accepted him with love and elation.

Soon the door chimes announced the arrival of more family members: Aunt Bianca and her three girls. Bianca embraced Dante and hugged him closely. For a time, she wouldn't let him go. She looked up at him, and again the amazing resemblance of Dante to their brother shook her, as it had the rest of the family. They all felt the same as Grandma Gaetane: Nicholas had finally come home! She introduced Camilla, her oldest daughter; and the twin girls that Dante wasn't even aware of, Lilly and Larra, who had just celebrated their sixteenth birthday! Camilla worked with her father Bruno in one of the three family-owned trattorias in the city. She did some of the cooking and serving, and the twins were in the tenth grade in a prestigious music academy in Rome. They were both recipients of scholarships and were studying violin. This was an amazing reunion! He hadn't known what to expect, as Aunt Felicity had never shared her negative feelings for the family as she remembered them. This was far more than he had ever imagined! A real family here in Italy! They were eager to hear of his plans, and they asked what they could do for him.

Grandma Gaetane woke up at the sound of the door bells chiming. Dante had been sitting beside her, and so desperately wanted to be able to thank her for the Villa and express to her how wonderful it was to meet the family. With skill, Lilly quickly and quietly translated Dante's words. When Grandma heard the words "Villa Val di Pesa", her face broke into an enchanting smile. She too had memories of years gone by with her family at the Villa, with everyone swimming in the pool or sitting around the covered portico while a campfire burned. She remembered young Nicholas playing the violin and Steophano trying hard to accompany him in song! She remembered Michaelo, her young husband. They were married in 1894 when he was nineteen and she was seventeen. She recalled her parents, the Ferraras, from whom she had been the sole heiress of a sizable amount of land, large investment holdings, as well as the Villa. She remembered the winery and the days of hard work, and the joy of coming out to the Villa on weekends and holiday time. She remembered all of this as if it were yesterday. These clear memories that she hadn't considered for a long time gave her warm pleasure.

Plans were made for them all to come out to the Villa. He looked forward to meeting his other two uncles. Sophia had a couple of days off, and it was decided she would go with him and help him choose his first vehicle to travel around the Villa. After spending two days in Florence, Dante decided on a brand new 1963 FIAT Campagnola Jeep, bright yellow in colour! The two of them laughed as they drove it back to Sophia's home.

He told her that when his friend Paolo came from Milan in a few weeks, he planned to buy a sports car. I mean, he lived in Italy now, and had a few plans of his own, in regards to his "financial standing".

CHAPTER TWENTY

RESTORING THE VILLA

FELICITY'S VOICE WAS CONCERNED AND ENQUIRING AS SHE SPOKE to Dante on the phone that evening. She had worried about how he would be welcomed into what she remembered as a very strange and eccentric family. Did they know his name? Did they call him Dante, or was he still "the boy"? He assured her they called him Dante, and that he was made to feel very welcome, and he told her that he was looking forward to meeting his two other uncles. He told her that his friend Paolo had met him in Milan and was coming in two weeks to stay at the Villa. Then he described the Villa. Felicity was ecstatic that things were going well, and she felt a deep peace come over her, knowing that Dante had been received well by the family.

Uncle David got on the line and Dante thought he heard a deep weariness in his voice. He realized just how much this man meant to him. When Dante questioned how he was feeling, David replied that he was feeling great and not to worry. He and Kenshin were taking another trip to Kentucky to buy a few more horses. David admitted he was still amazed that what began as a side interest had become a lucrative business. Dante inquired about Uncle David looking for a young filly and a stallion for him. David said he knew what Dante would like, and to leave the choice up to him. They talked about getting Four Winds over to Italy, and his uncle assured him that he would look after all the details. He of course would wait till he purchased the two new horses and send the three of them together by steamship!

Then Felicity came back on the line to ask about his grandma. He shared how Grandma Gaetane mistook him for his father Nicholas, and no matter what anyone said, he was Nicholas to her. Steophano had shared with Dante that she had just recently been diagnosed with Alzheimer's. A definite change had become apparent since Michaelo had died. She had taken the death hard, and she hadn't been herself since. She had shared a very close relationship with her husband, and they had spent every minute together both at the Villa and in the townhouse. They were inseparable. After his death she had suffered deep melancholy. Most of the time, her thoughts seemed to be miles away.

Dante asked about Scott, Olivia, Kenshin, Eiko, and the twins. Felicity shared her worries about Olivia, who seemed more withdrawn. She rarely came to the farm, but did keep in touch by phone. Dante said he would call Olivia in a few days. He admitted he was anxious to start work on the Villa. His immediate plan was getting the stables ready. He told them about his yellow Jeep, and the fact that he planned on buying a little sports car. Uncle David suggested one of the Italian-made Ferraris, an Alpha Romeo, or even a Lamborghini! Dante laughed and said he would be taking his friend Paolo along to help him purchase his first car. Both David and Felicity were overjoyed that things seemed to be going well for him!

Time flew by quickly for Dante with so much to do and such a feeling of accomplishment as he and Aldo estimated the projects that needed to be done at the Villa. One of the first things they worked on was the pool. Dante was able to clean out the leaves, but hired a pool company to replace the filters and liner. In three days, he had his pool ready for swimming. As he took his first dip in the pool, he pictured in his mind how it would have been years ago, when his father was young, and all the family were there, appreciating the pool. He was enjoying every minute of this.

The next project was firming up the stables. He needed to replace a couple of stalls and clean the old saddles and harnesses. When he was finished, in his mind's eye he could see Four Winds in his new home! Then he would start repainting the shutters on the Villa!

His cousin Maria came out for a day, and noticing the empty house, volunteered to help him pick out some furniture. They drove to a high-end store in Florence and spent the day purchasing the essentials, as she called them. They bought a large dining room table and eight matching chairs, a bedroom suite, a television, a leather couch and two matching chairs, and as Maria suggested, a few small tables and lamps, and a striking oval area rug in bright colours of lime green, brown, and burnt orange to decorate the main room. She also helped him choose sheets, blankets, and towels. She was an enjoyable young woman. At a later date, she said, they would go to the Uffizi Gallery and maybe find a couple of small oil paintings just to give his room some colour and ambiance. He did remember that he had a few posters from his baseball days, and he thought of putting them up, but a couple of oil paintings would probably be better for the main room!!

He asked Maria why the family had quit using the Villa and she replied that actually they had used it, right up until Grandpa died. Grandma Gaetane refused to go out to Val di Pesa without him. They had moved a lot of the furniture into the house in Florence, and had given some pieces to Maria and Sophia when they left home and moved into their separate apartments. As for the Vespones, Aldo and Doneta, they would live in the suite of rooms over the garage, for the rest of their lives. If Dante ever came home to Italy to take over the Villa, and he didn't want them there, then the Castrinni estate would provide for the Vespones finacially as long-time friends as well as employees of Michaelo and Gaetane.

Dante was only too glad to have Aldo and Doneta, and he appreciated both of them. They were old friends of his grandparents and family, which naturally made them friends of his!

Again, the thrill of being in Italy and in his own villa hit him as if he'd lived there forever. A large truck from the store followed them home that night to deliver the furniture, and his bedroom took shape within the hour! Dante was pleased with Maria's help. He hadn't exactly known where to start with the furnishing of the house, but realized that his bedroom was on the first of the list. The Villa had five other bedrooms, so he knew that this wouldn't be his last trip to buy furniture. He kept the room with the canopied bed just as it was. Who knows? Maybe one day Grandma Gaetane would be able to come and see the Villa herself!

Aunt Felicity and Eiko were both great cooks, but he had to admit that "Italian cuisine" was something else to consider! Doneta spent hours in the kitchen making dishes that of course Dante had never heard of. He couldn't even pronounce their names, but they were outrageously good! Fettuccine gigi, polenta, spaghetti, carbonara, and of course pizza! He had never been a coffee drinker, but espresso and cappuccino were growing on him daily. Doneta and Aldo consumed it at an hourly rate it seemed, and it was always fresh!

The next few weeks were busy for Dante. Paolo Russo came and spent almost a month at the Villa, helping Dante with odd jobs around the yard and the stables and looking over the grape vines. They spent three days looking at cars, and then they returned to Milan, where Paolo knew of a 1953 Ferrari 250 Europa coup, slate grey in colour. It had belonged to an older lady that Paolo knew and it had very low mileage. It was ten years old but just like new with soft dove grey bucket seats and a standard shift. It had been in a storage garage for the past ten years and hardly ever driven. There were so many cars to choose from and he could have his pick, especially when money wasn't an issue. Paolo was surprised when Dante chose the Ferrari, but he did admire his choice. It was a classy car!

Dante was busy! Bringing the Villa back to its original form was his main objective. He hired a crew of men and they worked diligently in the expansive grape arbour, as well as the olive grove. He worked for many hours in the stables, bringing in electricity and creating a new tack room. He was excited, as he was expecting the horses to arrive soon.

The day came and all three of them arrived safely — Four Winds, Fury, and Jasmine! Again, with the help of Aldo, and one of his neighbours, they fenced off a parcel of grassland to be a grazing pasture for his horses. He knew they would love their new home, as much as he loved his!

It was not his intention to start up the winery business, but he knew how unkempt it was. It looked pretty bad. Then he was approached by a young couple who were interested in the grape arbour. They had just moved to Florence, and had a small villa not far from Val di Pesa. Their land bordered the grape fields. He gladly made a deal to rent it to them.

CHAPTER TWENTY-ONE

DANTE TRAVELS

As Dante surveyed all of his accomplishments over the years, he was deeply gratified. With the help of Aldo and Doneta, he had a beautiful home he was extremely proud of.

He had been busy almost every day since he had arrived in Italy. He decided it was time for him to travel, and familiarize himself with his new homeland. Plans were made based on advice and ideas from the family, particularly Uncle Steophano, who had filled a small spiral notebook with his many suggestions.

He visited Rome, Venice, Florence, Lake Garda, Amalfi, and Capri, spending a few weeks in each city. Depending on where he was, he would drive or fly back to the Villa, check in with the family and the horses, and go riding and make sure all was well. He spent two months in Portofino, a fishing village on the Italian Riviera, just south of the city of Genoa. The port was fronted with colourful buildings and houses, and many super yachts in the harbour. He often visited Castello Brown, a sixteenth-century fortress and museum of art. Many of the pieces had been created by local artists.

It seems that anyone who travels finds a "favourite place", and for Dante it was Camolgi, a small fishing town tucked into the west side of the peninsula of Portofino, in the province of Genoa. He often found himself returning to Camolgi. The beaches were clean with fine, white sand. The weather was hot and he found it a great place to relax. This is where he really became fluent in the Italian language. "No English spoken here!" He now felt he had developed sufficient command of the language to have a serious conversation with Grandma Gaetane.

On one of the few days he was back at the Villa, he received a call from Aunt Mimi, his father's youngest sister. She was a surgical veterinarian responsible for over two hundred Arabian horses under the charge of Prince El Amari, who lived in the main port of Jeddah, on the Red Sea. The city itself dated back to seven A.D. Many of the old homes had actually been built from sea coral. Mimi was also an esteemed equestrian rider who competed in different parts of Europe. Dante and Mimi talked about horses for over an hour. He told her about the refurbished stables, and the arrival of his three horses. She, in turn, told Dante about Midnight, her coal black Arabian stallion. Dante assured Mimi that there definitely would be a home for Midnight at the Villa, if and when she ever needed one.

Aunt Mimi was eager to hear all of his news, especially about Grandma Gaetane spending time at the Villa. Just as they were saying goodbye, she invited Dante to come over and see her and the horses. He needed no coaxing, and was quickly aboard a flight to the International Airport in Jeddah, Arabia.

He loved Aunt Mimi. They had so much in common. He was welcomed into the palatial holdings of Prince El Amari and his family, as well as the stables of the Arabian purebreds he owned. These horses were more than impressive. They held their heads high with a distinctive head shape and high tail carriages. Dante learned from Mimi that these horses had a different bone structure, with one less rib bone, one less lumbar bone, and two less vertebrae. Quite amazing! He enjoyed being with her for various birthings, and he was delighted in seeing the little colts get up on their hooves, immediately walking and hungry!

One day, Aunt Mimi got a frantic call from Martin Burke, a colleague in Beijing, China. He was a practicing vet. Huan Chow was a ten-year-old old boy suffering from a rare form of cancer. Huan Chow's pony, one-year-old Li Wei, had stumbled and broke her front leg. Usually a pony is put down with a break like this, but the family pleaded with the vet to do anything possible to save Li Wei's life. As Mimi was a reputable surgeon, he wanted her assistance in putting in a rod and enclosing Li Wei in a harness for healing. Mimi and Dante were on a flight within six hours of the call. The operation went outwardly well. All three of them prayed the healing would be successful, and Li Wei would be free from pain. Five months later Mimi would hear from Martin that the operation had been effective. Li Wei was able to bear weight on her leg for a few hours each day, making the prognosis what they had prayed for. As a result of that, Huan Chow, his little owner, was also doing better!

While in Beijing, Aunt Mimi and Dante toured part of the Great Wall, spent some time in Tiananmen Square in the inner city, and visited the zoo to see the panda bears. When Aunt Mimi flew back to Jeddah, Dante took a short flight over to Tokyo. Again, he was thrilled at the sights around him. And of course, the food. He was becoming quite a connoisseur of different foods! He thought longingly of Kenshin and Eiko Akira who had enticed his appetite for Japanese dishes when he was a child.

From Tokyo he boarded a flight to Los Angeles, California to attend the wedding of one of his Dodgers' friends. During the ceremony, as the couple sincerely made their vows to one another, he realized he had never had a real girlfriend. Dates yes, and he had met some very nice girls, but never the "one!" Wow!

The flight home to the Villa was just as exciting, as if he were travelling to another holiday. He loved his home, and everyone in the family was excited to see him.

About a week after he had settled in, Maria and her fiancé, Romigi Balistore, whom they all called Rom, invited nine or ten of their friends out to play ball. They had talked about this for over two years, and thought it was time to start. Most of the guys were old schoolmates of Rom's. They had a great time. At the end of the game, they asked when they could come again, and so weekends became baseball. Rom and Dante spent well over a week clearing a parcel of land just beyond the old olive grove. They hauled in some sand and turf, and viola! A field!

The small pick-up team grew swiftly from ten to twenty-five. Weekends were especially busy and seemed to involve every member of the family. The teams played, their friends came to watch, and it was remarkable! It seemed that the fan base grew weekly. Rom was undoubtedly the most committed of all the team and the designated captain, as well as a first-rate catcher. Dante loved pitching to him. There was a good understanding between the guys not to be intimidated by Dante. He didn't always pitch. They were all aware of his injury, and knew that he wouldn't be throwing hard to avoid risking further damage to his arm.

Uncle Steophano decided he didn't like sitting on the ground or hauling out chairs or benches, so he bought the lumber and the guys built some bleachers. Rom teased Uncle Steophano that the next thing would be lights. Uncle Steophano didn't know if he was serious or not.

The games were drawing a lot of response from the immediate family also! Sophie told Dante that never had family ties been so enjoyable. Yes, the family got together for special occasions and holidays, but there often seemed to be no real connection. This was different. There was laughter and genuine merriment! It seemed the family was becoming more "down-to-earth", as the saying goes!

Aunt Elena and Aunt Bianca often came out during the week, and they enjoyed sitting around the pool and portico. They were there to help Dante furnish the Villa, but at no time did they ever interfere with his plans or ideas. They never imposed, and he was always grateful to have them. One afternoon he saw his aunts getting out of their car with what seemed to be some large paintings in their hands. On closer look he realized these were splendid oil paintings. Aunt Elena explained the paintings had actually belonged to his parents, sent as gifts from Michaelo and Gaetane, but the Carringtons had given the paintings back to the Castrinnis after the funeral. This statement from Aunt Elena was not accurate. Steophano had directly asked for the paintings. They were valuable. But Elena didn't want to imply anything negative in regards to their former relationship. One day, in the future, Dante would hear the truth concerning the strained relationship, and how it really was. But not today! Today was for building ties!

The largest painting was of the port city of Genoa, and featured brilliantly coloured houses bordering the water and many boats anchored in the harbour. Another painting portrayed a family of four walking down a path, with the wind blowing wildly at their clothes. The painting of a violin and a long-stemmed white rose was so exquisitely well done you felt you could almost play the violin and smell the rose. And finally, the smallest of the oils was of the Villa Val di Pesa itself. It had been painted over one hundred years ago, and given to Grandma Gaetane as a wedding present from her father, Marco Ferrara, along with the actual Villa. These were treasures to Dante, knowing they had hung in his parents' home in Toronto when he was a child, and before that in his father's home, when he was a child. This was another connection to the parents he could not remember.

Elena and Bianca would often bring Grandma Gaetane out to the Villa. She never said much, but she seemed to relax just by watching everyone. Elena found an old tape cassette marked "Nicholas, age ten, playing the F. Mendelssohn Symphony No. 4 in A Major at the Theatre Malabari in Venice." Five students in his age group had been invited to perform. Grandma found this quite amusing, and as she listened to the tape playing, she would glance over at Dante and smile! Dante was astonished and pleased at hearing his father play the violin at that early age. They often wondered, as Grandma Gaetane quietly regarded her family, just what her recollections were.

Time passed quickly and there was always something to do around the Villa. The twins Larra and Lilly were first-rate riders. They tried to spend as much time as they could at the Villa, on the weekends. He was only too glad for their company.

It is true that everyone was happy and contented. Aldo seemed revived at doing little odd jobs around the Villa. He enjoyed the laughter and chatter of the many persons who visited there. Doneta was probably the most satisfied of them all. There were guests to feed every weekend! As an excellent cook, she was in her glory. What greater pleasure could a cook have than to try new recipes and cook for many! And there was the love of cappuccino! This had become one of Dante's greatest delights. Back home in Canada and in the U.S., he never drank coffee! Never! But there was something about sitting down and sipping a cappuccino that seemed so right!

One of the most surprising moments came when Uncle Marco Pacorro asked if he could try playing in the outfield, and of course they let him. The twins cheered him on when he had a couple of errors in the outfield. When he came up to bat, they covered their faces. They were utterly shocked when he hit a home run! Although he had never played a game before, he too was falling in love with baseball, or maybe it was the comradery that was shared on and off the field. He came out most weekends, as his restaurants were only open Monday to Friday for breakfast and lunch. He and Camilla never failed to bring out amazing desserts as well as pizza.

Uncle Bruno Bethini, the lawyer, wasn't interested in any kind of sports and quite honestly, not very interested in anything but his work. At the urging of his wife, Elena, he managed to get out once in a while to watch a game and of course partake in some of Deonta's cooking. He had to admit he was enjoying himself. On one occasion he told Elena that he was beginning to realize how far away he had positioned himself from the family. He had never had anything to do with Uncle Steophano, and now they usually sat together to watch a game. You would often see them, with their heads together, discussing certain plays, and carrying on very animated conversations. Now Bruno felt he was getting to know his girls better, and restoring his relationships in a much better way. Both the girls were living on their own, so their paths didn't cross all that often. But it seemed different now!

Sometimes Dante almost felt guilty in regards to enjoying his life. He loved his family and was truly thrilled by how they'd embraced him. He was able to converse fairly well in Italian, and had some good conversations with Grandma Gaetane, but she still thought of him as "my Nicholas".

He understood the family members were deeply committed to their church. When they stayed over, they always drove into Florence for mass on Sunday mornings. However, they had never asked him to join them.

He had started attending a small church on the outskirts of Florence called "The Way", and he tried to go to the Bible study on Tuesday evenings. He wasn't known here as a pro baseball player, but just a nice young guy who loved the Lord. It was at church one morning that he noticed a stunning young woman singing in the worship team. She had a remarkable voice, and was beautiful to look at. He made it his business to find out what he could about her.

Her name was Cappi Geonna, and she was a resident pediatrician at one of the major hospitals in Florence. As he drove home, he became very conscious of the fact that this was the first woman he had ever felt an attraction to. He wondered just how he could get to know her better.

The next day he had a perfect opportunity to share his faith when Rom asked him if he had ever felt resentment or frustration at having to leave the Dodgers. Dante was actually surprised at the question. He had never considered these feelings in any way. When asked why, he told Rom that his life was in the Lord's hands, and he trusted Him to guide his path, whatever he was doing.

He shared how he had made a personal commitment to Jesus Christ when he was in the first grade, and had trusted Him from then on! These words were not unusual to Rom. He told Dante that he had been brought up Roman Catholic, but often he attended a small church on the outskirts of Florence with his friend Domonic.

Dante asked him if this church was called "The Way", where he himself attended. It was, and Rom admitted the words of the preacher had many times touched his heart and made him question himself in regards to his own life!

And, yes, he knew Cappi Geonna fairly well, and as the story goes, she was a cousin of a friend, of a friend, and they had met at a New Year's gathering just last year! She was smart and fun to be with, and would Dante like him to invite her out to a game? He smiled and said, "What do you think?"

It would be a while before Dante met Cappi. The next afternoon he received a call from Kenshin Akira to come home, as David Carrington had passed away.

CHAPTER TWENTY-TWO

HOME FOR A FUNERAL

Felicity looked out over the snow-covered yard and nestled down deep under the covers. David had been getting up early and riding down along the river bank on one of his new horses, Mexican Dude. He had brought him back from a trip he and Dante had taken in Kentucky a couple of years ago. The first snowfall hadn't stopped him from riding the big black gelding. He said there was just something captivating about riding in the early morning, over the crisp snow-covered ground. Felicity didn't mind, as long as she could keep warm in bed. She would often use that time, in the quiet dawn of a new morning, to thank her Lord for the blessings of life, and for the salvation He had given them. She would pray for those close to her, and intercede for the cry of God's heart to see "every tongue, every tribe, and every nation" come into the family of God. At times she would cry out for her only daughter, and her husband, forever asking the never-ending question of what had happened to change Olivia into the deeply troubled woman she was now. Upon rising, she started the coffee, knowing David would return soon.

Time went by and no David. Again, she looked out the east window of the kitchen and was shaken to see Mexican Dude standing by the barn doors, reins down at his side, and no David. She wondered if he was in the barn. Sudden alarm spread through her. She grabbed her coat and boots and ran towards the big horse. She quickly mounted, and turned him down the field road. There was no sign of David. Her heart beat frantically as she reigned the horse around and began retracing her steps.

Then she saw him, about a hundred yards down the section road, face down in the snow. After dismounting her horse, she gently felt for the pulse in David's neck; there was none. He was not breathing. She knew her beloved was gone! Her instincts told her that this was probably a heart attack. She knew he had been gone well over an hour, because she knew when he had left the house. She cradled him in her arms for a long time. She caressed his handsome face, wanting to keep that in her mind; she spoke to him quietly, telling him that she loved him and that she would be all right.

She told him that her love for him was a gift that she had always been amazed at, and would treasure, till they would meet again, as she knew they would. She held him close and told him that the years they had spent together had been so perfect, and absolutely wonderful, and because of their relationship with Christ, she would be all right till that great day when they would meet again.

As she held her beloved in her arms, she heard the sound of the old truck, and looked up to see Kenshin and Eiko. It was time to take David home. Kenshin lifted him into the truck, and Felicity rode Dude up to the barn. Grief comes to individuals in its own way. Kenshin cried out loud, and Eiko was speechless.

A call to the funeral home in the city was made, and then to Olivia. Felicity dreaded that call, but it had to be made. She talked to Scott first, and he broke the news to his wife. Felicity cold hear Olivia scream, and then cry, "No, no, not my Daddy!" Scott came to the phone and told Felicity they would come as soon as they could.

It wasn't long before the hearse came out to pick up David's body and take him to the funeral home. Felicity worried that Olivia would be upset not to see her dad, but she allowed the funeral directors to take his body. She marvelled that she somehow got through the next hours. Kenshin took over, and placed calls to David's parents. He left a message for Dante to call home.

They were all worried about how Olivia would handle the circumstances of her father's death, considering her intense reactions to situations. It proved to be a disturbing time when she finally arrived. She was incredibly upset about her dad, and angry that Felicity had let the funeral director take him away without her seeing him. She began to cry hysterically, and Scott had to take her upstairs to lie down. Again, she was angry at her mother!

David Carrington had been what you could call an icon of some sort in the circles he travelled. He was known for honesty, integrity, fairness, generosity, and friendliness. When the news of his passing broke over the little town and surrounding district, people were grief-stricken. As always in times of grief, friends and family were quick to bring comfort to the family, and in this case, it started immediately. Friends and neighbours called with meals, baking, flowers, and prayer! Dante was met in Regina by Eiko and Kenshin, who were openly grieving. Felicity was having a hard time. She was especially concerned about Olivia, who hadn't spoken to her mother since the news of her father's death.

There were many friends and business acquaintances of David's that attended his funeral. A group of horse breeders from Kentucky and North Carolina arrived to pay their respects to the man who had started out as a business associate, and over the years became a friend. Six close friends, including Kenshin and Dante, spoke affectionately and fondly of their relationship with David Carrington.

Olivia was given opportunity to share, but she declined. She was distant and standoffish during the time with friends and left early from the funeral with a migraine headache. Felicity quickly realized she would not be able to get through the coming days without the close support of Dante, Kenshin, and Eiko. The following Monday morning Felicity, Olivia, Scott, Dante, Kenshin, and Eiko gathered in the main living room for the reading of the will with their friend and lawyer, Michael Gallo.

Kenshin and Eiko were given the title of the home that David had built for them, including a small portion of the farm acreage. The couple were in tears when they heard this. Kenshin realized a valuable principle written by Paul in the Book of Galatians 6:9: "Let us not become weary in well doing, for at the proper time we will reap a harvest if we do not give up."

Felicity was left a large, undisclosed amount of money, investments and bonds, and the title to the big house. Olivia was given the total income from the sale of the Thoroughbred horses David owned. Dante's name was not mentioned in the will. Before Michael began reading a few minor bequests, Olivia stood up and ran out to the car, calling to Scott to take her home. This time, Felicity was not up to going after her. Dante followed Scott out only to hear him say, "I'm so sorry, Dante, I don't know what to with her anymore. I love her, but I can't seem to reach her, and most of the time I don't understand where she is."

CHAPTER TWENTY-THREE

CONFRONTING OLIVIA

Everyone was concerned about Olivia; she had reacted outrageously to her father's death. Dante couldn't understand the fact that she had stayed away from the farm and her mother. He knew Aunt Felicity was deeply wounded in regards to Olivia, at this time of mourning her husband.

Two days after the reading of the will, she hadn't been to the farm and hadn't even called Felicity or Dante. It bothered him significantly, so that afternoon, he went in to see her.

When she came to the door, she looked pitiful. Her hair was uncombed and she had bitten her fingernails down to the quick. He was, he acknowledged, feeling an undercurrent of real irritation and annoyance as he followed her inside. He had always been easygoing with Olivia. He had comforted her, and told her it wasn't God's way to be so angry, but he knew he had always indulged and pampered her. It was like walking on eggshells! Everyone around her wondered why there had been such a drastic change in her personality from when she was a young girl. She was not a happy camper, as the saying goes. She was pouty and very negative, and desired to be in control of those around her. He was tired of watching her hurt Felicity. He was well aware that Olivia hadn't shown her rudeness in front of David, as much as she did to her mother.

This time, rather than put his arms around her, he just stood looking at her. She knew something was wrong. He faced her with two questions: "What is wrong with you? Why are you so disrespectful to your mother?" He asked her to be honest just this once and try to identify the root of the problem. What had ever happened between Olivia and her parents to cause such a hatred, and did her feelings concern him? He surely knew it wasn't Scott, because this bitterness had started years ago. What had happened?

Olivia didn't like it! She didn't like being confronted.

She sank down onto a big chair and started crying, not wanting to talk. She told Dante to go away and not bother her. This was just a bad day for her. But this time he didn't listen. He removed his jacket and sat down facing her. He wasn't leaving until he knew what was going on. He wouldn't go back to Italy and leave his aunt, in the depths of mourning her husband, to deal with this girl. If this meant he had to move home to stand by Felicity, he would do just that. Olivia kept glancing at her watch, knowing that Scott would be home in a couple of hours. She didn't want to be venting her dark murky feelings in front of her husband, although she knew very well that he was aware of her mood swings. He waited. She continued crying. He waited. Once he looked at her, with her head down in her lap, and simply asked her to ask the Lord to give her clarity on what had started this bitterness in her heart.

She raised her head and quipped scornfully, "How would He know? He doesn't care about me anymore." He started to say something but she cut him off. "Look at the will! Can you believe he left the whole farm to Kenshin? He wasn't even family. Why would Daddy leave the farm to him, and me a bunch of horses that I have no interest in? Why? I can't even be around them." Her eyes were flaring and in her hatred, she screamed loudly, "The farm should be mine!" Dante really couldn't believe what she was saying! He had been at the reading of David's will, and was well aware of the contents.

"No! This could not be because of the will. This started years ago," Dante challenged her.

She looked at him and in a quivering voice said, "Your name wasn't mentioned in the will. Doesn't that upset you?" Again, he was speechless. He wondered if she had heard any of what their lawyer, Michael Gallo had said to her.

He was well aware that the income from the sale of the horses would be Olivia's. She would be free to pursue the sale immediately or in her own time. Did she have any idea of how much this would be worth to her? Did she have any idea of the value of David's horses? Obviously not. Just exactly what had she heard? He waited until she calmed down and asked again, "What is the real problem, Olivia? What is the underlying issue? Whatever started this?" She looked up at him and moaned pitifully. He told her, in no uncertain terms, he wasn't leaving until they got to the bottom of this.

She began speaking irrationally, and again he waited. She looked at him and said it began years ago, this moodiness and desire to control. She felt deprived, as a child. She was very limited in her activities, because of her allergies, and wasn't able to join in with the regular activities of kids her age. They teased her. She didn't like it. Did Dante remember when she had allergies so bad that he had to put drops in her eyes at lunchtime every day at school, and the kids made fun of her?

She had to have her hair cut short because she was allergic to her own hair. The kids teased her unmercifully! "Do you remember that?" Then when Dante left home to play ball, she was lonely and bored and her mother said no to a couple of Olivia's suggestions of activities she had wanted to do. She was angry at her mother. Without intent, she went into Dante's room one day, and just for fun looked in his top drawer. There she found two bank books, an investment certificate for a lot of money, she couldn't remember how much, and then it looked like a deed of some sort to a house in Italy. No one had told her about any of this. Dante was favoured and she was left out of the loop. She was angry because she saw him playing ball and living an exciting life, but she wasn't allowed to do anything because her mother worried so much about her allergies! She felt like she had been left out of the loop, and it made her mad. She wanted to be in control! She liked nice things, and yes, her parents were good to her, but she had no vision of her future. She just wanted to get out of the house and be in charge of her own life.

Her mother had insinuated that maybe she suffered from "depression" because Grandfather Towers, Felicity's father, had suffered from depression.

Just the word "depression" made her angry and not in control! It made her really agitated! To top it off, her parents were continually pressuring her about going to university or into nurse's training like her mother.

"Look at your friend Marlene; she has plans for her future," they said. They were always at her, and they were upset when she took the job at Eaton's. She also thought they were disappointed about her running off to get married.

Crying uncontrollably, she told Dante that she hadn't quit her job, but got fired because of owing money for enlarging the diamond ring Scott had given to her. She had also talked Grandma Price into signing the house over to Scott and moving to the retirement home.

She had been speaking loudly, but suddenly she became quiet and she was very still for a few minutes. He just waited. As she began to speak these truths out loud for the first time, she felt uncomfortable. For the first time, she felt embarrassed. She felt remorseful. She remembered Grandma Price bowing her head as Olivia explained how hard it was for Scott to live in their little apartment. There was not enough room! Yet all the while she knew that he had never complained about that to her, ever! She began to realize how she had pressured Grandma Price about the house. She had asked Scott for one hundred dollars, insinuating it was to go toward painting Grandmas house, when really, she needed it go towards her four-hundred-dollar account at Eaton's. She had never told Scott this. Taking Grandma's car in Missoula. Lying to her new friends about having a driver's licence. She thought about the car accident in Missoula, and the resentment she felt towards David after that. She thought about how she had acted at her dad's funeral, and at the reading of the will. She was very still for a time, seemingly struggling with something else. Finally, looking over at Dante, she said, "I went into your room one day, just after you and left for the States. I looked in your desk and opened up two manila envelopes, and found out about your savings accounts, your investments, and a deed to your Villa. Dante, I don't know what came over me, but I lost control and nearly ripped up the deed. I sat on your bed and felt rage come over me, and in the middle of that, I knew my reactions were totally wrong. I could never hate you, but the feelings were so ugly. I was furious that no one had shared this with me. I know that is wrong, but we always shared everything together, and I was angry because you didn't tell me about something so important. Why didn't you tell me about it?" she questioned.

She was genuinely searching now, and he answered her. "Your mom and dad never even told me about my inheritances. Olivia. They said they wanted me to follow my dreams, and not be influenced by my inheritance. The money would always be there for me. They looked after me like I was a son, and you know that. There was never a need for me to know then. I have never felt they were wrong in their decision. Just before I left for Florida, they took me aside and told me. Michael Gallo had looked after the investing. I'm grateful for their wisdom, Olivia!"

With her eyes closed and tears running down her flushed face, she suddenly recalled the words Marlene had shared with her years ago! Amazingly, they came back to her in crystal clarity, almost word for word: *"Why do you blame things on your parents? They are great parents. Why do you resist authority? You have a temper; you always want to control things. This will always keep you from a close relationship with our heavenly Father. This isn't how Jesus would want you to act, Olivia, and you know that."*

She remembered how her dad and mom were so concerned about her future, and how she would not listen to them. She knew the truth. She had been resisting authority all her life. She couldn't handle teasing or criticism. She did like to control things. And now, finally, she acquiesced. She gave up! She admitted her feelings weren't good. She understood them to be wrong! She would change!

She looked at Dante with confusion in her eyes. She was quiet. He didn't move or get up; he just kept looking at her. Finally, he said, "It's not enough to admit it, Olivia. You have to acknowledge it as sin and ask God to forgive you. That's the only way you'll be free of this resentment and jealousy." Her eyes were closed, and she seemed to be really thinking. Her thoughts overwhelmed her. It all sounded so easy, but would it work?

"I have left God out of my life for a long time." Her thoughts were in an uproar. She still wished Dante would leave!

Then she asked, with sincerity, "How do I move on from this resentment? How do I avoid being stuck in these feelings of hurt, and of anger? I've been like this for a long time. I feel it. How do I forgive, when I really don't feel like it? How can I change myself, Dante?"

Wow! Something profound was going on here! Dante silently asked the Lord to give him the right words to help Olivia. "I think we do it by faith, and obedience, Olivia. Forgiveness usually goes against our nature, so we forgive by faith, whether we like it or not. It isn't a feeling; it is a choice we make. We trust God to do the work in us, so the forgiveness will be complete."

She still didn't look up, but she had quit crying and seemed to be listening. She asked, "Do you really believe that, Dante?"

He replied, "Yes, I do. I believe God honours our commitment to obey Him, and our desire to please Him, when we choose forgiveness. Our job is to continue to forgive, by faith, until the work of forgiveness is completed in our hearts. Forgiveness doesn't mean you automatically forget; it means you lay it down and trust God. Does that sound complicated, Olivia? It is a matter of choice!

"In the book of Philippians 1:6, the Bible says, 'Being confident of this very thing, that he which hath begun a good work in you, will perform it until the day of Jesus Christ.'" Dante continued, saying that forgiveness is our path to freedom.

She was sitting very still, and he knew she was considering every word he said. He was quiet. He had said enough.

How can you possibly explain the power of God's Holy Spirit at work? She could not, but for some reason, she realized that only God could be revealing these thoughts to her. Only God could cause her to be honest enough to observe and understand her distorted outlook and her way of thinking. Only God, by the power and the gentleness of His Spirit, could identify this deep feeling, and call it sin!

She responded to His quiet call in her spirit. She asked Him to forgive the way she had treated her mom and dad, and to forgive her manipulating of others so she could have her own way. She was very still, as if she were pulling up different scenarios in her mind, and realizing the extent of her sin, and the harm it had caused to those she loved. To forgive her for lying to Grandam Carrington, for taking Grandma's car in Missoula, lying to the girls about her licence, and how she treated her parents when they found out. To forgive her for hiding the truth from her husband, Scott; and to forgive her treatment of pressuring Grandma Price in regards to the house. She asked Him to forgive her feeling of jealousy regarding the Akiras getting the farm. She thanked God for the horses, which had been left to her from her father. She confessed how ashamed she felt, after finding out the wealth she would incur at the sale of them. She asked Him to forgive her for hurting the ones she loved the most, and for pushing her relationship with God and her childlike love of Jesus to a lost corner of her heart. God hadn't changed or given up on her. She didn't know how she knew that, but she knew it. She spoke the words out loud, but the result was something she would never be able to put into words.

It was like a crystal river of pure truth ascended over her. She felt a heaviness that she had walked and lived in for many years being removed as if some invisible hands were taking off a floor-length garment and replacing it with a much lighter one. One that fit!

She cried softly now, and Dante was very still as the spirit of God touched his cousin. He just sat and waited, and finally she looked up at him. Her face was still red and puffy. Her hair was a mess, her fingernails were still bitten, but her eyes were sparkling and clear. Now, he stood up and hugged her closely. Both of them were amazed at what had just happened. Dante prayed and thanked the Lord for the miracle he could visibly see on her face. She was still in a place of utter astonishment and amazement. They sat quietly for a while. She shook her head, and wondered out loud how she could possibly face her mom, Kenshin, and Eiko. "God will be with you," Dante said, "and maybe when the time is right you could explain about what has transpired this afternoon." He told her that they would be able to see a change, and they would know it was God. She agreed, but she also knew she wanted to go to Scott, her mother, her grandparents, the Akiras, Grandma Price, Wilma, and Marlene and personally ask their forgiveness. She remembered the disappointment on the faces of her grandparents in Missoula. She literally shook her head at her outrageous behaviour, and asked the Lord to forgive her. A serious apology to them would be coming. She just knew she needed and wanted to do that.

It had been a while since Dante had put his arms around Olivia, but this time it was so right!

CHAPTER TWENTY-FOUR

CAPPI GEONNA

DANTE FLEW INTO FLORENCE AND WENT DIRECTLY TO HIS CAR IN the airport's parking lot. He had been away for over three weeks of rejoicing and spending time with Aunt Felicity, Scott, and Olivia. Olivia was something else! It was a miracle! Her whole personality and even her face had been transformed. Really! This was identifiable to everyone around her. Her conversion was from the heart, and the change had been observed by everyone around her. She looked so peaceful. It was hard to believe she was the same girl. His heart rejoiced over Olivia. She had followed the promptings of the Holy Spirit. She had gone personally to those she felt she needed to, and asked forgiveness. Aunt Felicity seemed overwhelmed by the change in her only daughter.

She and Dante had helped Felicity with various details and instructions Uncle David had left in his will. When Michael Gallo gave Olivia an approximate value of the sale of the horses and the breeding rights, Olivia was dazed! It was a staggering amount of money, and it was hard for her to receive it, because of her previous feelings and actions. David had sold most of the farmland, except for about twenty acres the two farm houses were built on. That property had been given to Kenshin and Eiko. Olivia had felt such resentment towards Kenshin for receiving what she considered "the farm", not knowing that most of the land had been sold years ago when David had invested everything into the Thoroughbreds.

She knew she couldn't change the past, and she still felt the anguish of her guilt from time to time. But for God! She was forgiven and she knew it. Yes, there were times when she remembered her actions; but she also knew that to dwell on the past would do her no good! He had died for her redemption, and she was very much aware of that. She had been forgiven and was created anew because of her relationship with Christ!

As Dante drove up the incline to his villa, he was taken aback by the number of cars parked alongside the driveway. He could hear the shouts of enthusiastic fans, and as he got closer to the field, he could see there were more players! Rom had predicted that people would come out just to see Dante, but he hadn't been there for well over three weeks. As he parked his car in the garage and walked closer to the field, he heard an incredible "smack" and wondered who was pitching. It was fast and it was hard! The sound of the ball hitting the catcher's mitt echoed in his ears. Who was that? He stopped, trying to identify the pitcher, but he was sure he hadn't met him before. He was a fairly tall guy, and had a smooth delivery! Clean! Dante just stood and watched as the pitcher struck out the last batter and retired the inning. He listened to the fans clapping and cheering in rapid Italian!!

Looking up, he recognized Sophia, and was pleased to see Uncle Steophano and Aunt Elena were just finding a place in the bleachers. He walked towards his uncle and was just about to sit down when he saw her, that stunning beauty, sitting in the bleachers and concentrating on the game. Cappi Geonna. Doctor Cappi Geonna, if you please! He stumbled down beside his uncle, who immediately embraced him in a bear hug, as he usually did. But Dante's eyes never left Cappi Geonna! He doubted if he had ever seen a face as radiant and beautiful as hers! He remembered the first time he saw her, how he had reacted, and was surprised at his feelings. He had never been interested in girls, and there had been a lot of girls, from city to city, and ball game to ball game!

She was spectacular! He wondered how she got here. Who brought her? Was she with anyone? "Where do I go from here?" he asked himself silently. Finally, it occurred to him. After all, this was his home, his villa. He certainly had the proprietary rights to introduce himself to her, didn't he? He was just thinking about how to approach Cappi when she stood up and moved ever so quickly in front of whoever was sitting beside her. She seemed to be approaching Dante. At the last moment, she held out her hand to Uncle Steophano with a smile on her face that could light up the universe! She was well aware that Dante stood close by, and he wondered just what Rom might have told her. Then her hand reached out to his, and she introduced herself in faultless English.

"Dante, I'm Cappi. A good friend of Rom's." He took her hand in his and hoped she couldn't hear the racing of his heart under his shirt.

"Yes, Cappi, I'm so pleased to meet you!" And at that moment, at the touch of her hand in his, twenty-five-year-old Dante Castrinni fell in love with Cappi Geonna. Yes, just like that!

He had never had a romantic relationship with a girl. But that was then, and this was now! This was not a girl; this was a woman. He was not a boy anymore. He was a man! This would be a story of its own.

Later, it was Uncle Steophano who invited Cappi over to the main house for some snacks and drinks, and she accepted his arm. Amazing smells were wafting out of the kitchen, and Dante was sure tonight was pasta faggioli, freshly baked bread, and his favourite cannoli. There were jugs of iced lemonade and tea. Doneta had prepared far more than mere snacks. This was closer to a full-fledged gourmet meal!

Aldo was moving the outside furniture around the big fire pit, making a place for all to sit. It all seemed unreal to Dante as he watched Uncle Steophano, moving about making everyone feel welcome. He was in his element, and enjoying every minute of it. He watched out of the corner of his eye as Uncle Steophano made sure Cappi was settled in a good location before the fire. Then, Dante wasted no time in joining her.

It seemed Cappi had been asking Rom about Dante also. She had noticed him at church, and as the old saying goes, she thought he was "a looker". They sat together around the fire, picking at the Faggioli, but neither one of them seemed hungry. He would gaze at the fire, and she would look at him. He was handsome. Totally Italian! Good looks, beautiful skin, and black hair. She, on the other hand, displayed a very pale, clear, shiny complexion with glossy, black, curly hair. Her eyes were a deep Purple Indigo. He remembered playing in Denver, Colorado, where mountains were described as "purple mountain majesty". That pretty much described Cappi's eyes to a T! This was an eye colour he had never seen before. Absolutely captivating!

Later, as he walked with her towards her car, he wondered just what the future would hold for them. Oh yes, he knew it would be "for them!"

Uncle Steophano was waiting for Dante after Cappi drove away in her car. He smiled when he told Dante how Nicholas, Dante's deceased father, had met Merrin Towers, just sitting at a sidewalk café in Venice. Nicholas had immediately fallen in love with her, and married her just a few months later! Steophano looked wistful as he shared this story with his young nephew. He remembered how the family had treated Merrin, and how they were so disappointed that "the boy" would not be raised in Italy with his family. Regrets? Yes! Looking back, Steophano had lots of them. He was definitely aware of that! But Dante was here now, and thanks to the loving care of the Carringtons, he was "the greatest kid in the world".

As Dante walked up the stairs to his bedroom that night, he had another "Italian" on his mind in the person of Luca Gabrielle, the young pitcher he had watched earlier. Dante hadn't even met Luca yet, but he would certainly be checking him out!

Just like that, Dante and Cappi were an item! It was obvious to everyone; there was no way to hide their feelings for each other. He had asked her out for dinner the day after they had first met at the game. Before the Chianti was poured and the carbonara was tasted, he knew he would love her forever! He marvelled at his feelings for her and hers for him! Love is amazing! He had never felt this kind of love before, but he recognized it immediately. He loved Cappi Geonna! From the very beginning, they talked easily. It was like they had known each other forever, and yet they had so many questions they wanted to ask each other. Cappi also very quickly recognized her feelings for Dante. It was just there! To define it, as Cappi would find herself saying in the coming years, "We feel so connected! So on the same page." Every day was different now. He had Cappi on his mind! Romance, something that he had never considered, had gone from possible, to probable, to factual! He was in love, and so was she, and the fact that she was such a baseball enthusiast didn't in any way interfere with his interest in the team. Cappi readily embraced all of his family. Her family had recently moved to France to be with the aging parents of her mother, and she missed them, so the Castrinnis filled a gap in her life.

Cappi would be finished her residency in a few months. At that time, she would move into a group of offices on the San Jacopo Boulevard, where she would be a full-time practicing pediatric physician. But for now, she was on call regularly, and if she were out watching a game, Dante would often see her, after receiving a page, get into her little sports car and drive away. She cared deeply for her little charges. Her work was heartbreaking at times, absolutely, but more miracles were won than disappointments. She would often find herself, especially during the night, standing quietly by a little crib and hushing a crying baby, or walking the floors while caressing one, if she had the time. She would lay her hand on the tiny bodies, and offer up a silent prayer to the Great Physician she knew so well.

CHAPTER TWENTY-FIVE

ALL ABOUT LUCA!

As for Luca Gabrielle, that was another story! He was nineteen years old, and was one of three sons, working with their parents on a large farm that produced sugar beets, corn, tomatoes, and lemons. This produce would be trucked all over Tuscany to many of the local establishments in Florence. He was six foot one, muscular, and "quite a looker", as the twins described him! He was a well-built, well-mannered young man. He had played a little ball in middle school, but that was a long time ago. Over the past months Rom had become fairly well-acquainted with Luca and his father. Rom was the Loan Manager in the Merchant Bank, where Lucas' father conducting his dealings. He had gotten quite familiar with both of them during various transaction in the bank. He knew Luca to be a level-headed young man.

Rom had invited Luca to come out and check out the team, and so Luca had just drove out casually one Thursday evening to watch a practice. Seeing Luca in the stands, Rom had called him onto the field, asking if he'd like to take a turn at the plate and try to hit a few balls. Luca didn't need to be coaxed. He grabbed a glove, picked up the bat, and quickly stood to the left of home plate. He hit a few balls. Rom watched him bat for a while, and then asked him if he'd like to try pitching a few. As he threw his first few pitches, Rom watched many of the guys on the sidelines move in closer to watch. Rom was a good catcher himself, and so he knew a good pitcher when he saw one. He could hardly wait for Dante to see this kid pitch!

When Dante watched Luca pitch, he knew he was good. Maybe better than good. Wishing he had a radar gun to time the pitches, he decided he would get one and check this kid out! He might just make the big leagues, if he desired this!

Dante called Luca aside after watching him one evening. "You're good, Luca! You could be pro." Luca laughed as if Dante was teasing him. "No, I'm serious. I timed you tonight. You are throwing at an average of ninety-five miles per hour. I've timed you on several occasions, and you've pitched at ninety-four, and ninety-five, ninety-three, and ninety-five! Amazing! That is better than good. What do you think about pro ball? There's a great team here in Italy!"

Luca laughed and said, "I'm for the Yankees, Dante; only the Yanks!" He was not joking, and Dante easily remembered his own boyhood love for the Yankees.

Rom and Dante talked seriously about Luca's skill. They both agreed it was hard to believe his speed and delivery; as well as his style and control. Game after game, when he was pitching, it was often a shutout, and when his team won, it was because of his pitching. Yes, they had a couple of good hitters, and Luca himself hit some good line drives, but nothing could compare to his pitching!

Baseball had never been Luca's first love. As he told Dante, "I played a bit in school, but that was over five years ago. Nothing serious." Now, it seemed he was just a natural on the mound.

Uncle Steophano, who had never even been in close proximity to a ball field in his life, or ever watched a game until this year, became quite animated when talking about Luca. He maybe didn't know ball, but he knew the kid was good. He seriously felt that Dante should do something about this kid. Luca was outstanding, wasn't he?

There had been recent visible changes in Steophano Castrinni. Everyone noticed it! He was tall man, quite thin. He had a few lines creasing his forehead and dark curly hair with a touch of grey appearing at the sides. He was in excellent physical shape, as he swam every day, and biked around Florence on his ten-speed. Actually, he was quite a good-looking gentleman now that a grin seemed to occupy his face, rather than the usual frown he had worn for so many years.

He had always been a very serious man, and no doubt would have been described by every member of his family, especially Grandma Gaetane, as "seriously severe". Not very approachable! Old friends would describe him as smart and intelligent, but oftentimes very aloof and reserved. His unapproachable and sullen character had become cheerful, while revealing a natural appreciation for his life.

Dante's arrival had touched the lives of every member of the Castrinni family in a remarkable way, especially all of the uncles, but most of all Steophano. He had experienced a personal transformation when his young nephew entered his life. Who can say? But now, to see Uncle Steophano, Uncle Marco, and Uncle Bruno watching a game was quite comical. They had never been more than courteous to each other during all the years they were acquainted, and only on special occasions did they ever get together. Bruno, Elena's husband, had never had much to do with the family. He was a busy lawyer, and seemed to have an excuse to miss any family gatherings. Now they were sitting together, avidly talking with one another, and laughing, seemingly in agreement, on whatever they might be talking about. Grandma Gaetane, who was usually very quiet, did not always engage in the flow of the conversation around her. Yet she was known to be observant at times, and she had frequently noted to her daughters how the family had changed since Nicholas had come home. She still acknowledged him as Nicholas, and the family didn't try to change her mind. She was especially pleased at the transformed relationship between her two sons-in-law and Steophano. It was clearly evident to all of the family.

Dante was perplexed about Luca, as he didn't seem overly excited about the game. But he seriously considered the training and advice that Dante and Rom were coaching him with. He heeded every word, saw changes in certain areas, and finally, he began to relax and enjoy the game.

Cappi was graduating in a couple of weeks, and Dante was trying hard to think of something outlandish to do for her! Once again, Uncle Steophano entered the scene with an "absolutely incredible, marvellous, idea. Why not take her to New York City for a few days? I'll come along as chaperone. We can see a couple of shows, and she can shop, and we'll take Luca over to see one of your buddies associated with the Yanks!" Just like that!

Dante couldn't help but marvel at his uncle, and the fact he mentioned the Yankees! He really seemed excited over Luca's pitching! Dante really wasn't one to jump into things, or was he? "Was this a possibility?" he wondered. He made a couple of phone calls to Myron Davis, one of the pitching coaches on the Dodgers, and asked his advice. Myron assured Dante he would get hold of one of the scouts, and have him call Dante. He left it there. If the scout called, Dante might pursue this idea, but if not, he would let whatever happens, happen. A call came two days later from Lenny Dreger, who called Dante in regards to this information from Myron. Yes, he would be interested in seeing Luca, but because of his personal schedule he couldn't get away for at least two or three weeks. He really didn't sound very interested, so Dante let it go.

Three days later a call came from Guy Browning, one of the general managers of the Yankees. It obviously hadn't taken long for that kind of news to be made known in the circuit! He more or less said, "Dante, if you think he's got something, then definitely I want to see him. I'll be over!" And over he came.

Nothing was mentioned to Luca, but because the games were just pick-up, there wasn't always a guarantee every player would be in attendance. Remember, this was a volunteer pick-up team just out for fun. Guy Browning and his wife Jenny flew into the Aero Porto di Firenze in Florence three days later. They were met by a smiling Dante and guess who? Uncle Steophano! After getting them settled in a nearby hotel, uncle and nephew drove back to the Villa. They had promised to pick up the visitors the next afternoon. Hardly a word was spoken as they drove, with each considering the various scenarios that could take place! It was Rom's job to make sure Luca Gabrielle would be at the game the next day.

CHAPTER TWENTY-SIX

A SCOUT FROM THE YANKEES

THIS WAS THE DAY! GUY AND JENNY BROWNING WERE WHISKED out to the Villa Val di Pesa in time to enjoy a tasty luncheon served by Doneta. Most of the family were there. Conversation was interesting as Guy had some great stories about Dante's career, and as he said, he'd have liked Dante to have been with the Yankees!

Around four-thirty in the afternoon cars began driving up the graveled incline to the Villa and parking along the side. Fans were seen entering the bleachers; some brought their own chairs and others carried blankets to sit on, as if at a picnic. It was a warm evening and the wind was just blowing enough to move the stately cypress trees and keep everyone at a comfortable temperature. Uncle Marco was ready for the crowd that day, with roasted peanuts, containers of cold lemonade, and crushed ice for everyone!

The previous evening, after thinking it over, Guy had called Dante. Instead of watching a game, as Dante had planned, he said, "Let's just watch Luca. That's what we're here for."

Dante agreed. "Let's just put him through the paces!"

When Luca came out that afternoon to play, Dante took him and the rest of the players aside, and explained that a scout from the New York Yankees was in the stands and wanted to see Luca in action. No game today! This would be "all about Luca". It was decided that Rom would catch for Luca. The players backed up to watch.

Excitement filled the air, although those in the stands didn't really know what was going on.

Luca took the mound. He was quite emotional! Who wouldn't be? What was going through his head? In the past few months, playing baseball had been at the top of his list. He loved it. He really couldn't believe this was happening!

All the dreams he never thought would be his could come true; they were sixty feet, six inches away!

Taking a deep breath, he composed himself and set to deliver his first pitch. He looked at Dante, and knew that Guy was behind home plate with the radar gun. He cleared his mind and just pitched.

The first pitch was ninety-four MPH.

The next pitch was ninety-six MPH.

He continued to throw a variety of pitches, including curves, sliders, and fastballs!

He was intense and totally immersed in the game. Guy was immediately impressed. He appeared to have his game well under his control, and in his mind Guy knew what he was seeing. A natural!! Just as Dante had told him.

He came down from the stands smiling, and said to Dante, "He is better than you said; maybe even better than you, Dante."

Dante answered him with a grin, "That's not all, Guy. This kid can bat, too!"

Dante asked Rom to catch for Luca. He crushed his offerings!

Guy admitted that Luca was amazing, "But how would he be with a major league pitcher? No offence to you, Rom." Looking at Dante, he grinned and said, "How about it, Dante. How about you pitching him a few?" Dante agreed.

Friends and family in the bleachers and on the sidelines tensed in anticipation. This was something they had never witnessed before. A New York Yankees' scout, here at the Villa Val di Pesa, to watch Luca Gabrielle, and now to see Dante, retired pitcher from the Dodgers, take the mound. Uncle Marco was so caught up in watching, he forgot to give out his roasted peanuts.

Dante threw a few warm-up pitches. Luca stepped into the box.

Luca smiled, but Dante had his game face on.

Luca took the first pitch to size up Dante.

The next pitch, Luca sent screaming over the left field fence.

Dante was thrilled that Luca hit the ball, but not because he threw it.

The next pitch, Dante dug deep and threw his best curve. Luca lined that to centre field, and Dante just smiled, and looked at Guy, who knew that he had seen enough to offer Luca a tryout with the Yankees.

Dante was triumphant, Rom was exultant, and Uncle Steophano was beaming. Guy Browning was more than impressed with the nineteen-year-old pitcher!

Guy was immediately on the phone with the Yankees manager, and announced that for sure they would be bringing Luca to the farm team in Florida for tryouts.

There was a rare excitement at the Villa that evening, and a relieved Uncle Steophano! He just knew that Luca was meant for greater things. He was real baseball material!! Luca's family had all come to the game that day, and were actually at a loss for words as they had watched Luca on the mound. His father, a big burly farmer, later enclosed his son in his arms, with tears running down his cheeks. He couldn't even believe what was happening. Luca had never mentioned any interest in baseball. He had played a bit with his high school team, but only during the scheduled sporting events the school sponsored. He had never said a word about baseball!

Plans were soon made for the trip to New York City. Dante and Cappi decided they would get married there. Aunt Felicity, Scott, and Olivia would fly to New York for the wedding. It was Uncle Steophano who made all the arrangements for the flights and hotel bookings. Cappi was thrilled beyond belief that she and Dante would be married at the famous Waldorf Astoria Hotel in New York City. After inquiring with her parents in France, she wasn't surprised that they wouldn't be able to join them for the wedding. Cappi's grandmother had recently fallen and broke her pelvis, and needed constant care. They assured Cappi that they were happy for her. They had met Dante on only one occasion, but they liked him very much. They knew their daughter and trusted her judgement in finding a husband. She assured them that the Castrinnis were a great family and had made her so welcome. She was especially drawn to Uncle Steophano, who actually accompanied her to Rome, where she purchased her wedding dress. He would be walking her down the aisle.

CHAPTER TWENTY-SEVEN

A TRIP TO NEW YORK

DANTE, CAPPI, STEOPHANO, AND LUCA, HAD TO WAIT AT LaGuardia for over an hour until the arrival of Felicity, Scott, and Olivia. Dante noticed that his uncle seemed a bit anxious, although he could be reading him wrong. Finally, he saw Aunt Felicity coming down the escalator, and behind her Scott and a smiling Olivia. He rushed to hug his aunt and cousin, shook hands with Scott, and then made the many introductions between Uncle Steophano, Cappi, and Luca with his Canadian family.

Felicity immediately went forward with her arms outstretched to Cappi. Out of the corner of her eye she saw the face of Steophano Castrinni. Over the past few days she had thought often about this meeting. Her memories of Steophano were not good ones, but she had kept all of this to herself over the years, never voicing a negative word to Dante. Introductions being over, they all moved out into the brilliant sunshine of New York City. Each probably wondered what the others were thinking.

Luca speculated about being picked up by the Yankees. Dante and Cappi thought about getting married, with his family present. And Steophano, what was he thinking? Would he remember the two times he and Felicity had previously met, each time leaving with very unresolved animosity towards each other? Steophano hoped for everyone's sake that all would go well!

After meeting the family, Guy Browning and Luca left immediately for a meeting with the managers. They announced that they would be back for the wedding. Dante had ordered a limousine to drive them to number 301 Park Avenue, the Waldorf Astoria, where suites had been booked for all of them. The wedding was to be held in the Dorchester Room just three days from now!

Scott and Olivia were awed by the skyline of the city. Conversations were unrestrained. Questions were asked and answered from the front seat to the back seat. It seemed odd, though! Uncle Steophano was usually right in the middle of most conversations, but he remained noticeably quiet. Aunt Felicity was full of questions about the upcoming wedding, and also about Luca.

Scott and Olivia were invited to be attendants at the wedding. Luca would be leaving for Tampa after the wedding, but until then would be very busy with Guy Browning and one of the Yankee managers. That seemed to leave Felicity with Uncle Steophano! At the same time, both Steophano and Felicity both appeared to realize they were going to be the odd couple, like it or not!

He made the first move, in saying directly to her, "You did a fine job, Felicity, in raising Dante. Like us, you must be very proud of him." This was the first time he had ever called Dante by his name, and she smiled graciously, accepting the deeper meaning of what he actually meant. She had made up her mind to let bygones be bygones and enjoy the next three days, with or without Steophano Castrinni.

It was hard to do! He was there every time she turned around, suggesting this or that, and answering to her every need. He was very sincere! Charming, in fact! She certainly hadn't remembered him as being polite or pleasant at all. Yet now he was attentive to her, as well as to the needs of Dante and Cappi in regards to the wedding ceremony. It seemed he and Cappi had everything under control.

Felicity contemplated her old memories of Steophano.

None of them were good!

Was he ever interested in Dante's life? No, he was not.

Did she remember him as being courteous? No, she did not.

Did she remember him as someone she wanted to get to know? No, she did not.

Did she remember him being so handsome? No, she did not.

Did she remember his blue, blue eyes? Absolutely not!

But here he was, paying the utmost attention to all of them, but possibly more to her! She really didn't know how to handle this; but, again, Felicity drew from her deep inner resources, and managed to be as delighted as she needed to be at this time. After all, it would only be three days until she would be homeward bound, and she was looking forward to spending what little time she could with Dante and Cappi.

He was sitting directly across from her in the limousine, and it seemed he couldn't keep his eyes off of her. She was striking, with rich blonde hair pulled back in a chignon, a straight navy blue sleeveless dress, and a fancy green and white scarf draped over her shoulders. Her feet were encased in very high navy blue thin strapped sandals and she carried a matching navy blue bag.

He didn't remember Felicity being so gorgeous! He didn't remember her being so eye-catching, and he certainly didn't ever remember being attracted to a woman like this! He was astounded at the rush of emotions that were roiling up inside of him. He tried to keep looking out the windows as the limousine silently advanced closer to the city centre. He couldn't! Steophano wasn't fooling himself. He was a mature sixty-eight years old. A confirmed bachelor. Absolutely, he was. Yet here he was in a limousine, travelling to New York City, with the most beautiful woman his eyes had ever seen! He didn't seem to be aware of anyone in the car but her!

He mused to himself, "Is this how Nicholas had felt for Merrin, and how Dante feels for Cappi? Love at first sight? Yes! He could certainly understand. Maybe it runs in the family! I wonder if this could be true for me or for Felicity." How could aloof, severe, and arrogant Steophano Castrinni be experiencing these emotions? He chided himself for even going there, remembering their past encounters. Yet he was wondering just how he could open up a line of communication between the two of them.

With shame, he remembered how they had treated the Carringtons while attending the funeral in Toronto, and the sudden trip to Canada to take Dante home to Italy.

He remembered it very well, and so regretted his attitude at those times! How to undo this, so many years later?

After getting settled in their respective rooms, the group of six joined for dinner in the main dining room. Most of the talk was about the upcoming ceremony, Cappi's dress, and what would be expected of each of them. Steophano was to give Cappi away; Felicity would light a unity candle, and Scott and Olivia would be their attendants. The only guests would be Luca, Guy, and Jenny Browning. A wedding breakfast would be served after the ceremony, and then the bride and groom would fly over to Niagara Falls, Canada, for a short honeymoon.

Before the coffee and dessert were served, the two young couples got caught up in the details of the coming day. They decided to go and check out the wedding preparations, leaving Steophano and Felicity alone at their table, waiting for their coffee.

It had to be now! Not wanting to miss the moment, he began by giving her condolences on the death of David, to which she responded affirmatively and thanked him.

He then began to tell her how sorry he was for the way he and his sisters had treated her and David on both of their previous encounters. He sincerely regretted how aloof he had been, even lying that the sisters didn't speak English. He regretted his audacity in stepping up to the dais at the funeral, when it had been arranged that neither of the immediate families would speak. He told her of the absolute positive changes in the relationships within the whole family since Dante had entered their lives, and how they were so grateful for the care and nurturing and values that had been poured into Dante's life. The family was so very proud of him.

He shared how they all respected Dante's belief in Jesus Christ. The family recognized how Dante relied on God, and drew life from Him! Steophano didn't mince any words... He was sorry for and ashamed of his actions. He took full responsibility in regards to his sisters' manners, as he had coached them very well. How foolish it was to fly to Canada and expect to just take Dante home with them. He felt embarrassment creep into his spirit, and his cheeks go red, as he spoke these words out loud. How foolish he had been. He told Felicity he wouldn't want to know how it might have been if they had taken Dante home as a two-year-old, those many years ago!

Finally, he asked, "Could you ever forgive me?" There it was, out in the open! Could she forgive him? Would she?

She did. It wasn't hard for her. Forgiveness was the basis of her belief system, as a committed Christian. She quickly grasped his deep repentance and regrets.

She didn't bring up how she had felt in the past. She simply said, "Yes. I do forgive you, Steophano. I do!" And she meant it. Emotions were highly present.

She continued, "But there are things that I want to ask your forgiveness for, Steophano. Many times when you sent the money for Dante, I was fearful of your coming and trying to take custody of him. We never told him about his inheritance until he left for Florida. Both David and I wondered why you never corresponded with him. Maybe I was secretly afraid that if Dante was aware of his wealth, he might leave us. I can't explain it, but I had many sleepless nights worrying about your motives, and I held a grudge towards all of your family. My sister Merrin shared with me how she was treated by your family on her first trip to Italy. I think I took her offence on myself. Even on the second trip, she realized things weren't right. I know she carried a deep sorrow for her husband's feelings in regards to his family not really accepting her.

"I am sincerely sorry. I ask for your forgiveness, Steophano. The day when you came to the apartment, I had been in Merrin's bedroom looking for clothes for Dante, and I found a baby book, and inside was his birth certificate. I didn't hesitate or think it over, I just took it. I didn't tell anyone until the night of our departure from Toronto. I had it all the time.

"Can you forgive me, Steophano? Would you?"

He answered affirmatively that yes, he would absolutely forgive her. Yes, he would!

He was relieved, to be sure, but this seemed too easy. There were twenty-two years of tension between them. Could forgiveness be that easy? He didn't think so. And yet he did not hesitate for a second to forgive Felicity for her feelings, for her judgments, and for hiding the birth certificate. He only wished he could go back and change the past, but because that is impossible, he began to realize that forgiveness is a gift that we can choose to move forward in our relationships. She was offering this gift to him, and he to her! Determined to move on, he thanked her sincerely. He reticently held out his hand, and she took it. He placed his other hand over them. Her face conveyed gratification as well as ease. He had meant every word, and so had she.

CHAPTER TWENTY-EIGHT

ANOTHER LOVE STORY

STEOPHANO ASKED FELICITY WHAT SHE MIGHT LIKE TO DO TOMORrow. He had numerous suggestions. He had already made a reservation for the Harbor Light Cruise, including an evening meal and a tour of the New York Harbor, Statue of Liberty, for the next evening.

Uncle Steophano had never been to New York, but he had studied his travel guide well in preparation for this trip! It wasn't the safest city in the world at this time, in 1970, and the city had been through so much! There were homeless people living underneath the Brooklyn Bridge. The underground subways had become unsafe for many travellers, and they were considered dangerous by many. The city itself was on the verge of bankruptcy, and Central Park had become known for muggings. He knew all of this, and had planned his tours and sightseeing with a very reputable tour agency.

There was no going out alone... he made sure of that. Being in charge of the touring, he had packed a lot into each day.

The next morning had all six of them up at seven, eating breakfast at eight, and into the limousine by nine. New York City was awaiting them! Steophano had taken charge of an all-day tour that included the Empire State Building, Yankee Stadium, as well as the recently built Madison Square Gardens. It was a full day ending with a horse-drawn carriage ride around Central Park. Dinner that evening was at The Barbetta, at 321 West 46th Street, a refined Italian restaurant that catered to Italian-born musicians.

The next morning shopping was on the agenda! Olivia and Cappi were having the time of their lives. Not needing anything, but considering a lot, they passed the day browsing in Saks, Macy's, and Bloomingdale's. Steophano was surprised when Felicity fell in love with a pair of shoes and a small handmade leather bag in a deep shade of burgundy. He watched her eyes as she examined the purse. It was made of the finest soft leather, just like the shoes. Inside was a label bearing the name of "House of Fendi". These items had been made in Italy!

He smiled when she recognized the label, and insisted on purchasing the shoes and purse for her. All the while she was explaining she didn't need them, he was striding to the cashier to pay for them.

That evening all six of them dressed formally for the Harbor Light Tour and dinner. A very American meal of roast beef and Yorkshire pudding was served with apple pie.

Music was provided by a string ensemble, and when Steophano asked Felicity to dance, she blushed and said she had never tried. He took her by the hand and guided her onto the floor. She found herself in his arms and moving toward a strain of music she had never heard before!

His arms held her securely, and her feet seemed to be following his without her even thinking about it! What on earth was she doing, out on a cruise ship, with Steophano Castrinni, on a dance floor, dancing, and feeling "thrilled" to be in his arms? What was going on here? Later, as they were strolling the deck and leaning over the railing looking at the New York Harbor, he desperately wanted to say something romantic to her. But, what to say? He was definitely out of his element here!

He desperately wanted to tell her how very beautiful he thought she was, and how he thought he was falling in love with her. And how he hoped his feelings would be reciprocated. Instead, he asked her, "Is forgiveness that easy, Felicity? What about how I made you feel? Can you really forgive that much?"

Her answer was the same: "Yes, I can, and I have, Steophano!"

He questioned her with "How? How is it possible?"

Her answer was as simple as before, "Because God forgave me, I can forgive you. It isn't a matter of feelings; it is a choice, and I chose to forgive. You have to accept my forgiveness." He did, but with perplexity! This was something totally new to him!

They were up early the next morning, and ready for the ceremony by eleven a.m.

Luca and the Brownings arrived just in time, and the Wedding March began promptly!

Cappi was picturesque! Dante still could not believe that, in mere moments, she would be his wife. How had God so miraculously brought them together? He silently thanked the Lord for this precious woman, and for the blessings that were so abundant in his life.

She came down the aisle looking radiant in a dress of pure white spun silk. It was floor length, slim-fitting, and had long sleeves with an open back. She carried a bouquet of white lilies and stephanotis, tied in pale pink and green satin ribbons. A veil covered her face and Steophano could feel her shaking as he walked down the aisle with her. His emotions got the best of him, and when he was asked, "Who will give this bride away?" he could hardly remember his reply.

"Yes, I do." Tears filled his eyes and he found it hard to control his emotions. This was a brand-new occurrence for Steophano Castrinni! He had never been out of control in his life!

Olivia was dressed in the palest of pink, and with her blonde hair, much like her mother's, she looked gorgeous! Felicity wore an ankle-length dress of the palest grey, she held a corsage of dark red arantherea orchids, on her arm was the Fendi burgundy purse, and her feet wore the Fendi burgundy shoes!

Steophano had to admit that Cappi Geonna was the most beautiful young bride he had ever seen, but in comparison, Felicity Carrington was utterly enchanting!

Later that afternoon Dante and Cappi boarded a short flight over to Niagara Falls, Canada for their honeymoon. Scott and Olivia had received tickets from Guy to attend a Giants game early that evening, and Guy and Luca were off to another round of meetings. Once again, Steophano and Felicity were left alone.

They had changed into casual clothes, as it was a warm evening, and they found an outside coffee pavilion. They seated themselves and ordered espresso. Talking seemed to come naturally. One thing led to another, and both were amazed at the unanimity they shared in their conversation. Both had questions. No doubt both of them were remembering the past, and how distinct and distant their actions, opinions, and feeling were! And here they both were, in New York City, really being very sociable, appreciating each other's company, and forgiven of their past responses and choices. This was absolutely amazing! For today, here in an open pavilion, things were particularly different and extremely astonishing! He was charming, and she was breathtaking! He was magnificent, and she was drawn to him in utter fascination!! This was New York City. People were milling and conversing all around them, loudly, but they were oblivious. They were acutely aware of each other.

With an inquisitive smile on her face, she was first to speak. "What are you feeling, Steophano?"

He wasn't bewildered or confused. He identified exactly what he was feeling. But he didn't know if she was in a place to hear him. Would this be too soon to be really truthful? Would she hear his heart, or remember the past that was between them? Would it be better to go back to Italy and maybe start a long-distance friendship, based on the congeniality they had shared over the past couple of days?

What to do? What to do? Suddenly a thought occurred to him as he remembered something he had heard his nephew say repeatedly, in many different situations. What was it now? Yes, he remembered. "When in doubt, ask the Lord." Ask the Lord? That was something Steophano Castrinni had never attempted to do, but he did it now, even wondering if God would hear him!

He asked how he should approach Felicity with what was burning in his heart. And he heard, very quietly, "Be honest." Be honest? Could that be God, or was it just his own mind, answering a cry in his heart? He listened and he heard the very quiet, but very resonating words again, "Be honest."

He responded accordingly, and said, "I believe I am in love with you, Felicity." His heart was beating so hard, he was afraid of the results. "I think it is love at first sight!" This was another old saying he was aware of. This was new territory for Steophano, who was always so well-prepared for anything he ventured into. Well-read! Well-versed! But, not today!

Her head was lowered, and as she raised her head to face him, he knew this was a definitive moment in his life, and the answer to this statement, whatever it might be, had the power to change his life, as well as eternity for him.

She looked at him square in the eye, as the saying goes, and spoke quietly, "Love at first sight, Steophano? That couldn't be for us. We met years ago."

That couldn't be for us! That was all he heard. His heart seemed to stop. He felt weak at the knees. The loud chatter of the crowds around him became suddenly muted. It was just him and Felicity. His heart fluttered.

She was talking, but he wasn't listening. But she was still talking. Her lips were moving. What in the world was she saying?

Then he caught only a few words, "I do love you, Steophano. It is a miracle. I do love you! I don't understand how this could happen. I believe it is real, but I too am amazed!"

He heard her... He heard her say, "I do love you, Steophano." He stood up rapidly and she was in his arms. He tightened his arms around her, certain he would never let her go. Her heart was pounding also. Here she was in New York for a wedding, and in the arms of a man she had disliked for many years. Was this a reality or a dream? Her thoughts ran to David, and his advice to her over the years... "God has a plan, Felicity. It's always good, and He never fails!"

She raised her head to look into his eyes, and he bent down to kiss her fully on the lips. "Can you believe this?" their minds kept asking. Uncle Steophano couldn't remember the last time he had kissed a girl. And yet, for some reason, he wasn't worried about that. He was very confident. He just took her in his arms and kissed her. Then he kissed her again... and then, she responded by kissing him back passionately. She felt his strength and confidence, and couldn't believe how safe she felt in his arms.

Again, his blue eyes were full of tears. He was so emotional. He couldn't shake it! He knew deep down inside that a relationship with Felicity Carrington would include God. He knew it. And from witnessing Dante and his relationship with Christ, he was well-versed in the facts, as he called them. "You must be born again."

He also knew that it wasn't the knowledge of facts that would decide this commitment. He knew it was a matter of his heart simply saying yes to Christ.

And with his mouth very close to her ear so she could hear, he simply whispered, "Lord. I have believed in you all of my life, but I have never made a personal commitment to you. I do this now. As I stand beside this woman, this daughter of yours, I do believe in your Word. I do believe that Jesus died for my sins, and I have been forgiven."

As she looked at him, it was now her blue eyes that teared up. She hugged him close, and realized once again how God does have a perfect plan for our lives.

Steophano looked again into the eyes of the woman who had totally captured his heart. He asked her, "Will you be my wife, Felicity?" Her answer was a simple "Yes."

Steophano told Felicity how Dante had made such a positive impact on their lives. He had learned to speak quite fluently in

Italian. One afternoon, he had shared the Lord Jesus Christ and the plan of salvation with Grandma Gaetane. She had listened intently, and responded with, "Yes, I will ask Him into my heart. I will!" And she did!

It was with great excitement that Grandma Gaetane had shared with Steophano how Nicholas (she still called Dante Nicholas) had told her the story of salvation, and that she had accepted Christ as her Lord and Saviour. Dante had influenced this family with his love, devotion, and simple trust in Christ.

Over in Niagara Falls, Ontario, not knowing what was unfolding in New York, Dante gazed at his bride, the beaming Cappi Geonna Castrinni, and he felt grateful for the life he was living. He had been orphaned as a small boy, had been placed in a God-fearing family, had received Christ as his personal Savior, played baseball for the Brooklyn Dodgers, met and loved his family in Italy, and married Cappi. He was grateful for all of these blessings, and knew, without any doubt, that in God, he had triumphed!

www.ingramcontent.com/pod-product-compliance
Lightning Source LLC
LaVergne TN
LVHW041632060526
838200LV00040B/1547